The Test of Love
Brothers for Life

By

Grace True

Grosvenor House
Publishing Limited

This book is published by
Grosvenor House Publishing Ltd
Link House
140 The Broadway, Tolworth, Surrey, KT6 7HT.
www.grosvenorhousepublishing.co.uk

A CIP record for this book
is available from the British Library

ISBN 978-1-80381-569-5
eBook ISBN 978-1-80381-570-1

Dedication

Praise the Lord, oh, my Soul!
Praise the Lord for He is Good!

I give thanks to the Lord
for my angels: Lawrence and Ophelia
And for a special friend.

Psalm 100:5
For the Lord is good and his love endures forever;
His faithfulness continues through all generations.

John 14:6
I am the way and the truth and the life
No one comes to the Father except through Me.

His grace, mercy and love endures forever.

Contents

Chapter 1
The dream

Today it was the 1st of March and the smell of spring was here. It was still cold outside but the sun was up and the flowers had started to bloom. So beautiful colours were around and the trees were green and bringing new life; baby leaves and lovely colourful flowers. At least some of them were near my house. I always loved spring: new beginning, new hope. And the smell of the grass in the morning, so fresh, always brought me joy and hope.

But for some reason today I felt tired and I was not in the mood for anything, and for sure not to meet Holly. It was Saturday, and I promised that I would go to her apartment and we would spend the day together.

This was me, spending some Saturdays with Holly. Well, said "some", as we quite often had arguments and then I had a free day; a day off to enjoy myself. Well, I was the peaceful one, but she loved arguing and "taking two for tango". It made me smile thinking of that.

It was 10am and I was lying in bed, bored of life, feeling with no purpose and thinking of a better future, and then when I found a few minutes of quietness, my phone rang. Of course, my girlfriend would not give me a break. I did not answer and got up slowly. I sat up looking at the clock and wished I would be somewhere else but not here. Surely she would call again. She always called and called, and lately I would not answer the phone.

At my age–35–my life was not bad, after all. Or was it? I was working as a manager in a car industry and my job was pretty good. And I had a girlfriend, Holly. True, she was some sort of a girlfriend, but not the right one. We were on and off for the past year or so. At least I was in a way settled. Before, I did not settle. She was number three. She was a pretty girl. However, something was missing in my life and I was trying to figure out what it was. My heart was wrestling and my mind flying. My heart was not satisfied and my mind bored. I wanted answers, enthusiasm, a life with love, fulfilment, joy, some sort of peace. And nothing of that I experienced, or had an idea what they were.

Maybe because I felt I was getting too old, I kept Holly; not necessarily that I even liked her. She was talking too much and bossing me all the time. I was not in love with her. No, love was something like a mystery for me. Probably I stopped believing that existed. At least not for me. Maybe I was more "special" or weird. Romance and all the beautiful things that would make your tummy have butterflies and the heart beat fast and your eyes sparkling of love and passion, was non-existent for me. Someone to share laughter and joy and smiles, and spend time together and have love quarrels, was far away in a dream land.

I wished so much to find true love, a lovely girl that I could give her my heart and her to mine but, well, it was just in a way forgotten for me.

I used to like to dream and think and hope for better, but the reality was always painful. I knew where I was.

Ah, let's not forget the visits to her parents each Sunday. It was worse than ever imagined. But her sister and mum were as bad as Holly and they were talking and talking good, that by now I used to start taking two paracetamols before going there to make sure my headache would not end up a double headache, as I would call it. It was really awful! They were talking, and me being there like the invisible man that nobody would notice – sad!

My house was a small two-bedroom house and I got lazy with cleaning. Well, I did clean, but could be a bit better. My clothes were everywhere. This was not me, but living with Holly and her life being a mess, I ended up a mess. I could not clean two houses. I was constantly cleaning her flat as she never did, and gave up cleaning mine as by the time I finished hers I was too tired to even move a finger.

As I took a shower and cold water woke me up, suddenly out of the blue a thought came to my mind. *What if I would have had a different life*? Well, I would if I could! But would I if I could? Then I laughed. I did have a good imagination! Me, having a different kind of life? That would have been amazing. My life was boring, and Holly was boring. She was not for me that was definitely for sure. I thought again of love. Love? You must be joking. I was not in love. I just had her around so I won't be alone.

Thinking seriously, I was alone even if I *was* dating Holly; I felt so alone even when she was around. My heart was lonely and lonely. But who would I share these things with? What kind of life could I have? Many of those thoughts were buried deep down in my heart, and when I was by myself I would dig up treasures and try to make my own world a better place. However, I would not act upon any; just put them back into my treasure box deep down in my heart. So me and me, just me!

My brother had his own life. Scott was not in the mood for me for sure. And he was working in the NHS, the big successful doctor, loved by everyone. That's what I always heard. Who could compete with my lovely brother? He was the big brother and I was the "naughty" little brother; the prodigal son. Not sure why my father called me like that. Maybe because he never liked me. Well, I was still going to family parties. Yes, I, Mike Davis, was needed when someone in the family needed cars and deals and ideas. Then I would be their best friend. Then I would be forgotten again and no phone call or messages for weeks. Yes, I felt so lonely; never wanted or accepted for who I was; needed for convenience to fill in blanks and do things.

But in all this messy world of mine, John was a true friend. John meant more to me than anyone. He was the one who made sense in my life, as nothing else was making sense at this point in time. With John I could be myself, and that meant so much to me. No one wanted to know about me and be part of my life but John proved himself a true friend. I really was treasuring his friendship.

One thing about John: he was going to his lovely church. And I was fine with that, but that was not me, oh no. I had enough sins of mine, and church was a bit scary for me. I felt that they might even hear my thoughts. But at the same time I felt so peaceful, and a hidden place filled with joy and something I could not explain.

The phone rang again and I got annoyed as I just came out of the shower and my thoughts got interrupted again. Holly was not very patient or considerate. Well, I promised to be there.

Finally, after dressing with a pair of jeans and a t-shirt, I looked into a mirror and my hair looked messy. Well, I was the handsome one in the family: big blue eyes and my light chestnut hair. Who would not love me?

Well, they loved me conditionally, but they did not think I was successful enough; good enough to be part of my father's family. More success, more love! In my family everything was about how much money you made. It was like a family meeting of competition and comparison. Well, I was speaking of my father's side of the family. Pete, my father, was living like one-hour drive from me in another town, and I honestly did not miss him. He and Mum have been divorced since I was young.

As I drove to Holly's house, I felt suddenly a feeling of sadness, compassion, and same questions came in my mind: *What direction is your life going? Can you change it? Why don't you move? Why are you stuck in the same place*?

As I knocked at the door, I knew what to expect, and she opened the door shouting, "You are a jerk, Mike, you know! Why don't you answer your phone?" A tall woman looked at me and she was angry.

"Good morning, Holly, nice to see you!" said Mike indifferently. Without looking at him, the woman with red hair and green eyes spoke with a firm voice, "We are meeting Mum today and we are going for dinner. I promised her."

Mike made a face, like eating a lemon. It was not the first time when she played him about, and knew there would come an argument if he said no. He actually did not want to go at all; today or ever again. He just put up with Holly and with her family. Looking at him, angry, she confronted him again.

"Don't tell me you are not coming! *Again*!" said Holly.

"You know I do not want to go. I do not know what you are even asking!" Mike was begging or giving up.

"Don't start or you won't sleep here tonight!" she said sarcastically, with her usual way to manipulate.

"You start again with this, do you? Why do you always want to argue? I don't even know why I date you." He said something he never said to her before. Coming near him, she put her arms around him and smiled.

"Well, you love me! And you need someone. Do you?"

He looked at her and realised, as many times, they were both on two different planets. "No I don't, Holly. I do not love you! For sure I do not need you!" he whispered. At least he had the courage to say it; probably, as he already admitted to himself, the truth. Now the truth was there and could not have been avoided. No, he did not love her. The truth had to be spoken. She turned around as she heard what he said.

"Mike, you are such a jerk, I told you. I should get rid of you. As my mum keeps telling me, there are men that make more money than you. I look pretty good, I could get myself anyone I would like to."

Mike was not in the mood for her chatter and stood up from the couch where he had landed with indifference. "Holly, I believe I better leave. I do not know why I even bothered coming by," and he started to walk toward the door, looking at the watch. It had just been 20 minutes since he came, and he was going. Holly changed her tactic and rushed in front of the door. Then she put her hands around his neck and started to kiss him on the face. He did not respond, and actually kind of gently pushed her. She kept modelling her body close to his. Mike put his hands on her shoulders gently and moved her out of the way.

"Holly, you should not even have asked me today to come if you knew you were doing one of your acts again. I am off. Give me a break for a few days. I definitely need a break from you."

As he walked out the door he heard her screaming with anger behind his back, and saying all kinds of words, mostly cursing him. She was pretty good at that. But that did not bother Mike any more. Something was happening in his heart and mind, and he did not really know how to explain it. He was really relieved that he left. Yes, he was getting back to his "planet", and smiled.

He entered his car, having a new perspective, and drove off. The moment he was in front of his house he received a text message:

Hey, Mike, do you want to come by for dinner tonight? Emma is cooking.

John.

He always messaged him at the right time.

Mike entered the house and sat on the couch. It was peaceful and he really liked that. It was really quiet. A, actually, it was very, very quiet. He closed his eyes and breathed, relieved. It was a perfect Saturday. It was peaceful, and a few birds were singing in one of the trees nearby and he could hear them. They were so happy. He lay on the couch and listened like this for some time. When he opened his eyes, he looked around and he realised his house was a mess: clothes downstairs, dishes everywhere, and he did not have time to even put the dishwasher on. He sent a message to his friend and said yes and yes three times. He loved visiting with John and his wife, Emma. They were the best things he had in his life; kind loving friends, always there for him. Of course there was his mother, Helena. She was a sweet lovely lady. Well, he loved her dearly and they were very close to each other.

He put some music on (well lately it was classical as it calmed his soul) and he decided to clean his house. That was quite something. He started with the kitchen and soon enough he was actually upstairs in the bedroom. He did a fantastic job, even cleaned the bathrooms and managed to put all the clothes away. His mum would have been impressed. He ended up in the bedroom, which was his last plan, and he was in a go, go mood, especially since he had a big bed full of clothes. By the time he finished he felt really good and proud of himself. He sat by the edge of the bed and another thought came to his mind. *How would you like to be without Holly*? You could date someone else; a lady that you will fall in love with and she will fall in love with you. Or take a break from dating.

Why are you dating Holly? That was an old thought that he had on and off sometimes. But today those thoughts were bringing him hope, peace, and he was meditating quite a lot. He lay on the bed, fixing his gaze on the ceiling, and with the arms under his head, he closed his eyes for a minute. Well, the time passed quickly and that minute became two hours and he woke up really late in the afternoon. He realised he slept so much. He was tired, as he was the other day working late and then had to do cooking for Holly. She never liked to cook. And yes, she did some sort of tidy up her kitchen, but that would not last long for Holly, would it? She would move things from one place to another and never put them away.

As he opened his eyes he blinked a few times and said out loud, "I can't believe this! I had a dream. I do not have many dreams. Incredible. I have to tell John. He might translate it for me. He is with God and dreams and angels and the Bible." He moved around an hour throughout the house, and by 4pm was finally out of the door. John was 15 minutes' walk from him and was easy to walk sometimes; better than driving. He loved fresh air, and spring, and walking.

When he arrived there he saw a car parked in front of his friend's house. He walked with confidence through the little front garden and then he noticed that someone was at the door already waiting.

He knew his way at John's house as he was often there and it felt like home. As he was walking he noticed a young lady with beautiful chestnut hair on her shoulders, and dressed very nicely. She seemed to have lots of books in her hand. As he approached, the steps made a noise and he said with a soft voice, "Hello, can I help you?" he asked politely.

She turned her head and she looked at him and said, "Hello, I am Bella, a friend of Emma's and John's."

"Hello, Bella. Emma talked about you. Glad to finally meet you. I am Mike!"

She smiled and spoke up, "Yes, Mike, thank you for your kindness," and he helped her with her books.

I looked at her and she seemed like a very kind woman. She was not very tall, probably 160cm, and had green eyes. A very gentle lady. She was dressed in a pair of jeans and a nice t-shirt.

The door opened and Emma said hello to everyone. "Hi, Mike. How are you? Did you meet Bella?"

"Ah, yes. We met." I looked at her and for a moment I felt an emotion in my heart. That was not me – to get emotional. Or if I did I was mostly sad. Probably this lady, Bella, made my day sparkling–shining in a way–and brought some light as I was caught too deep into my thoughts.

John came from the dining room and invited me in as well. As I followed him, our eyes met and she smiled and went with Emma, probably in the lounge. She made me curious, but I was sure I will have the chance to meet her again, as she was as well a close friend of Emma's as I was a close friend of John's.

"How are you, Mike? Did you not meet Holly today?"

Kind of waking up to reality, I sat down and looked at John. "Yes, I met her, and she wanted to take me to her mother again. And I just said no and left. Actually, I got brave enough and told her I do not love her and I am in no mood for arguing. So amazingly I spent my day at home. It was a good day."

John brought a cup of tea over and he sat at the table facing me. "Don't tell me you argued again?" He looked concerned.

"Well, I left. That is how we are doing it lately, so like this, I won't argue with her."

John did not say anything else as he knew the situation well enough as Mike was his best friend. He told him many times that he should find himself a nice girl, but Mike did not listen. So, John was very patient and unless Mike was bringing the subject up, he did not want to stress his friend. He did tell him that he was praying for him. And he did. He wanted Mike to meet someone who would bring love in his life and treat him much better than Holly.

"John, can I ask you something?" I was not sure how to start.

"Yes, of course. You should know that by now, Mike."

"I had a dream!" I looked at him and wanted to start the story, and Emma came by in the room, followed by Bella, and interrupted us in a way.

"Bella is leaving, but I invited her tomorrow in the afternoon. Hope that is OK, John?"

John was a tall handsome man with dark hair and brown eyes. He was very kind and so patient. He turned around toward his wife and spoke politely,

"Yes, of course, Emma, and it would be our pleasure. You are always welcome here, Bella, you know that!"

"Thank you, John, both. I will see you tomorrow." Then, turning toward me she said with her kind voice, "Nice meeting you, Mike."

I smiled and said, "The pleasure is all mine, Bella!"

As Bella was leaving, we moved into the lounge and I started to tell John my dream. It was really important to me, as not always would I remember what I had dreamed and was something that made a touch on me, an impression I believed was important, was unusual. "It seemed that I was on a dark road and it was night. And I was lost and kept wandering. I could not find my way, for sure. It was dark and I did not know if there were streets, or where I was. Might have even been a field or anything. Then suddenly in front of me a light appeared and out of the blue was an angel. The angel was shiny, white. Well, I do not know how angels are supposed to look, but this one was very shiny." I stopped for a moment, trying to remember and also focusing on all details of the dream.

"Go on!" John prompted me and listened with interest.

"He spoke to me and said, 'Follow the way, follow your heart'. Then I saw a church and I followed him as he showed me the way, and the angel said, 'You will find all your answers, and peace here'. And once I walked in, the angel disappeared."

"Interesting!" said John, meditating.

Mike was silent for a moment then, looking at his friend, spoke very direct. "I believe I need to go to church to find my answers!" John smiled and looked at his friend and waited to see what else he would say. "Yes, I know you asked me before. It was once last year. But that dream was so real for me. John, lately I had lots of questions coming to my mind. Yes, John, tomorrow I am coming to church. What time is it?"

John looked a bit shocked and was not sure how to react and what to say to his determined friend. "Mike, it is up to you if you want to come to church. This is the first time that I have heard you say that in a very long time. Your dream is true; Jesus gives you all the answers. He has the answers and what your heart is looking for."

"Yes, John. I want to come to church. I have been unsettled with lots of questions lately. Can I join you as I have no clue what to do?"

John raised his head and spoke kindly to his friend. "The church is a place of peace, love and friendship. Yes, we would love to have you with us tomorrow. Don't worry, it is not some sort of ritual. We are a lovely charismatic church and very friendly. Come as you are!"

Mike left his house friend later that evening very uplifted and with a hope and a desire to move forward in his life; to seek more and do more in his life. Some of us settle and get stuck and never get up again. We can get comfortable and the years pass and we lose the passion, the joy, the reason, the call in our life.

He felt more confident in himself and started to do things that he liked. He loved crafting small figurines and he sat down quietly in the lounge and put on some music. Actually, Emma and John gave him a very good CD with worship music for Christmas. So, music and crafting. He carved a lovely small bear, like 20cm or so made of wood. He had not been doing that in quite a long, long time, probably in a few months as he was always babysitting Holly. When he finished it after a couple of hours he had tears in his eyes. He never knew how much he missed doing that.

And yes, it was also his guitar. He was playing it sometimes, but Holly did not like his songs. He took his guitar and sat on the floor next to the carved bear and started to play a sad song. Tears came down his face and he didn't even know why he was crying. His heart felt touched by a new feeling–it was something new–and felt something was happening with him and in his heart but he could not explain it. He kept playing and he started feeling some peace. And he heard the worship music playing in the background as well as he forgot to turn it off, and tried to play a song along with his guitar. From tears, he turned to smiles and felt joy. Mike had a lovely evening and had a very good time in the end. He finished his evening with a beautiful movie, a comedy, and laughed again. Probably he forgot to laugh lately. So tears of sadness and tears of joy.

Going to bed that night, hope was more than a dream; was something that he was pursuing again. Somewhere, somehow it opened a door of a new beginning for him. The spring was in his heart and life, and was willing to go for it, fight for it, chase it and challenge himself.

He lay in his bed looking at the ceiling and listening to a few lost birds as they went to bed. His street was very quiet and a few passersby were walking quietly. The wind knocked at his window and a small wave of rain hit the window, and he smiled. It was quiet and he fell asleep as never before. He was in a better place, moving toward the impossible that would be made possible in Christ.

Chapter 2
Who are you?

Sunday, lovely day, spring and flowers blooming everywhere. The rain last night refreshed everything around and there was an aroma of drops of love in the air.

Birds showing up in each tree and making their lovely music were all part of a beautiful beginning of spring. The smell of nature waking up, it made Mike feel that his heart was waking up. There were two birds at his window that had a nest in one of the trees and they were there each year. Probably they never left. He loved to wake up listening to them. He felt refreshed and was ready for another day. He was looking forward to going to church. His mum would have been proud of him.

By 9.30am he was at John's door. He was dressed nicely with a shirt and a pair of trousers. He actually was very excited for his new adventure and was curious, actually. What would the church have to offer to him? And also he wanted to know more about the Lord. His mum taught him a lot of things, but as he grew up he did not choose the same path as his mum.

John was very nice and polite, and invited him in. "Hi, Mike. You look very good. Come in, come in. Emma is taking her time. You know, that happens when you are married. You need to learn patience." He smiled.

"Yes, yes! You know I don't! You two are a lovely couple and I know you for so long don't I, John?"

John looked at him and went back in time. "Yes, like 10 years or so. Remember we met in that car park when you helped me change my car tyre! You showed me kindness and grace, and we have been good friends ever since."

"Yes, of course. I can't forget." Mike smiled.

Walking from the dining room, Emma said good morning to Mike who was mostly walking around after John as he was getting ready.

"Do I need a tie or what? You seem so nice, dressed up, and makes me feel... I do not know," asked Mike, a bit concerned as he was not sure about his new adventure. The truth is he was not really crazy for ties and fancy coats, but he did have a shirt. He was wearing shirts at work so he had plenty of those. In a way he felt he was dressed for something special, and it was. Today was the day that the Lord has made, was his day, a day of spring in his life and a day of breakthrough.

"No, you look perfect, Mike. But I am helping with the prayer group at the end, so I like to look good at church for the Lord. Better than going shopping," he laughed.

Passing by her husband and Mike, as she was getting ready Emma looked at both and confirmed more than asking, "We need to pick up Bella. Her car broke down. She called me this morning. Hope it is OK if we all go in one car?"

"No problem with me, Emma."

A few minutes later we were all in the car. Finally they were ready, but to me it seemed like a lot of time just moving around. The church was a 20-minute drive from John's house and we stopped on the way and picked up Bella. As I was sitting in the back, she ended up sitting next to me, which I actually ended up enjoying more than I planned or thought.

"Good morning!" She spoke politely to all of us. She looked a bit surprised to see me, but John explained as I wanted to join them at the church service. I looked at her, and she had a lovely dress with red flowers and her hair was down on her shoulders. She had beautiful green eyes, a lovely smile and she smelled good. That thought made me smile. Probably some perfume. For the second time I felt a sparkle in my heart. She was so nice. And yes, being around another woman, just to say hi, was much quieter than being with Holly. It felt peaceful to be sitting next to her and I felt quite calm and relaxed. For a long time I did not enjoy myself like this: just enjoying a ride at the back seat next to a lovely lady with beautiful eyes and lovely smile and such a kind gentle voice.

The majority of my colleagues would have known me as "Speed". Speed for sure, as I always was on the go, go. Probably my speed of thinking and also passion and desire to help others was well-known among my colleagues and I was there when you needed me. I loved to move quickly, and probably for me was a normal speed and for others would feel like I was rushing. But that was me! And then when I was with Holly I had to do the majority of the things as she wanted to be served and she did not care at all. We are all different but also we can all be selfish and self-centred and not realise how wonderfully created we are and made in the image of a lovely Father, creator: God.

No, I did not feel loved by Holly. I felt I was convenient for her. I felt I was just there to satisfy all her pleasures and use my money for shopping. She was always buying clothes, and I being polite or stupid was paying for them. She was working part-time in a shop and was mostly all day long with her mother or her sister talking about everyone. That I found disgusting and for me was gossip. We broke up a few times and then as she begged me I took her back, and there you go – I could not get rid of her. But this time I believed deep down in my heart that I did get rid of her and something good would happen in my life.

Well my life was not quite happy. I was just living and plodding along; no sparkle, no passion, except when I was at the big shop I was managing. Cars – I loved cars and was quite good even fixing them. I was totally in love with BMW and was driving one. At least one thing I was doing good; I was working at the right place. Managing a car dealership with over 100 employees was not bad. I loved it, and we were not only selling and buying, but also offering a repair service.

"Where are you working, Bella?" I asked her out of the blue, with a desire to know more about her.

Bella turned her head and looked at me and spoke up with her soft voice. "I am a teacher. I teach at Westpark Primary school. What about you, Mike?"

"I am a manager at BMW – cars for you. I love cars." I had to add that as I did love cars.

John laughed and added, "You are very good with cars, Mike. And well said, you are crazy in love with cars!"

She smiled to me and added, "My car broke this morning and I do need to take it somewhere for repairs. My old mechanic moved away and now I need to find a new one. You might be my answer from the Lord."

I looked at her and felt really relaxed speaking to her. "Well, I guess I am sent by God. If you can wait till tomorrow, you could bring it to our repair shop. I can see if the boys have an opening time to take it in and give you a quote."

"That would be great. No problem, I can wait. Might need to take a taxi to the school."

Emma spoke. "I cannot help you tomorrow. I am early, out and about. You know, working in the NHS I start my shift at 7am."

Out of blue and without planning to I felt prompted to speak. "If you do not mind, I can take you to the school on my way to work."

"Are you sure? I do not want to cause you any inconvenience."

Looking straight into her beautiful green eyes I added with certainty, "I would love that, would be my pleasure, Bella!"

Unsure and a bit hesitating she agreed. "That would be great!" Thank you.

It was quiet and John, as he was driving, smiled and looked at Emma. Sometimes other people see what you do not see, especially if they are friends with you. They look after you in a silent way and pray for you, and wish and hope the best for you and with you.

"Does your car need to be picked up? Does it work at all?"

"Well, the engine does not even start. Yes, it will need to be picked up, yes. It is good you are asking. I am not sure what to do. Thank you."

The rest of the road I was quiet and just enjoyed the company of a nice lady who was not shouting at me. She looked good, she smelled good, was nice, beautiful and she was calm and had a soft voice. And you could have a nice chat with her – perfect! I just enjoyed the conversations in the car and looked out the window, lost a bit in my thoughts.

At church, finally, a beautiful building, and a few hundreds of people. We were not late, we were on time. There were lots of friendly people saying hello. For some reason I felt so happy and peaceful. I felt I was at the right place. Yes, a church became my right place, which had never felt like that before.

Probably I changed my heart, attitude and opinion about church. My mum, who was very dedicated to going to a small Baptist congregation, would have been really happy to hear that I went to church. I promised to meet her this afternoon and take her for dinner.

Bella went in another direction and gave me a shy look as she walked away. She was helping with kids groups and I went with John and Emma.

I enjoyed the entire church service. Even if I was not much of a singer, I tried my best and the songs were quite uplifting for me. I had no clue what I was doing, but I found it pretty easy to follow the rest of the people and felt quite relaxed. All seemed smiley and friendly.

The sermon was about *I am the Way, and the Truth, and the Life*. Yes, of course it was about Jesus, and George Lewis, the main preacher, did such a good job. Some things he said got deep into my heart and I was meditating at them.

"The Lord loves us and works in our hearts and lives. The Lord is good and kind. The Lord is always making a way, and brings the truth in every situation. Then He makes a new path, a new beginning. God is with us. If you let God work in your lives he will take you on a journey, and step by step He will lead you. He will open doors of favour and doors of grace. He will close doors for you. And even when you do not understand, He is with you. The Lord loves you too much to let you on the same path where you are. The Lord wants to help you and bring light into your life. Draw near to the Lord and trust in Him. Give to the Lord all your problems and ask him to make a way, and He will. The Lord's love never fails."

As I sat there, my phone started to vibrate. Of course, who else? Holly. She was a nightmare. And it would be my nightmare if I did not take action soon. I did not answer, of course. I really enjoyed the preaching. It brought me peace to my heart.

At the end of the service, it was prayer time and anyone who needed a special prayer was asked to go in a special area on the left of the church where there were chairs. And John was the one who was leading the prayers.

A few people already walked there. Some were standing and some were already seated in the chairs, and some others left quietly. Somehow, like in a dream, I stood up and went there and sat on a chair. I was not even sure what I was doing and why I was there. However, my heart prompted me to go and ask for prayers. Only God knew how much I needed him and I was a lost child trying to find my way in life drawing near to the Father.

I wanted to find my way, to move forward, and felt very lost, and confused and lonely, and needed so much God's love.

We were a group of about 30 people I think, and then as a beautiful instrumental worship was played quietly by the band, lots of people from the church came and started to pray in groups of two or three quietly for each person that came at the Lord's feet and asked for prayer support. I saw a lady coming toward me and a man.

"Hello, I am Maria."

"Gavin," said the man.

"I am Mike!" I introduced myself.

Both of them asked me what I would like to pray for. They were quite gentle with me and told me if I do not want to share it is OK, they understand.

Looking at them I just said, "I want Jesus to reveal to me things and show me the way. I feel kind of lost and confused." I guess we are all lost and confused, and Jesus brings us back to the truth, brings us back from the wilderness and makes a path and rivers and streams of water, but to me, this was just the beginning of the journey with the Lord.

They both asked me if they could lay their hands on my shoulder and I said, that's all right with me. They explained to me that they will pray for me, and they did. I closed my eyes and felt peace, and a few minutes later I felt a sparkle in my heart. They had such a beautiful prayer and I felt a river of love flowing in my heart. The lady said to me, "I had a vision for you, Mike. Would you like me to share?"

Surprised, I said yes.

"It was a book and the name on it was Mike. And a voice said, 'Who are you, Mike? Who are you'? And it was repeated three times, Mike."

I looked puzzled and did not understand, and Gavin spoke up.

"The Lord asks you, Mike, who are you? It means you need to discover who you really are. The Lord wants to help you find out your identity and your path in life. Follow him."

I thanked them both and then I spoke with a few more people who seemed nice and friendly.

On the way back, John and Emma took Bella and me back home. Bella was the first to be dropped off at her house and they offered to take me home too. As my mind was wrestling and thoughts of what Maria and Gavin told me, I asked John, "Do you mind if I ask something?"

"Of course, go ahead, Mike."

It did not bother me that Bella was there as I felt comfortable with her and wanted her to hear too. "I went for prayers today, and honestly I do not know why. A nice man and a lady prayed for me and they had a message for me. It was a question: Who are you, Mike? Not sure what it meant"

"The Lord wants to help you, Mike, guide you and show you His way." Emma was the first to speak and turned her head to me and smiled.

John was driving the car and agreed with his wife. Mike nodded and said, enthusiastic, "Yes, that is what they said too."

Bella looked at him and spoke with a kind voice. "Mike, if I may speak?" and she waited, and he encouraged her. "The Lord wants to help you find your identity. Who are you? It is not what you do. It is not what other people want or tell you to do. It is your heart. The Lord wants to know your purpose in life, your calling, your heart's desires, and to help you follow your heart. It is about who you are in Christ. Who are you?"

Mike looked at her and did not say anything. He had a deeper understanding of the question, who are you? However, suddenly he felt sad and the question kept hitting at the door of his heart. *Who are you? Who are you, Mike*?

He went home very sad, but he did not show his feelings to his friend John or everyone else in the car. He did not want his friends to worry. From all the people around him, John was a true friend, a friend in need, a friend all the time; not only in the joyful moments but in sadness as well.

As he entered the door, finally home, that moment his phone rang again for maybe the tenth time and he picked it up, tired. "Hello, Holly."

"Where are you? You—" and she kept cursing him.

"Holly, I was at church!" He answered with a kind voice and was very calm.

"Are you crazy? At church? Are you coming here? I am going to my mum and my sister. They are waiting for us."

For a moment, Mike felt the time stood still and a voice in his heart asked him again, *What would you like to do, Mike*? And like being woken up from a sleep, he said with same calm voice, "I am not coming, Holly. I am meeting my mother!"

"You cannot do that. You are not nice to my family, I keep telling you. I am not putting up with this anymore. I keep telling you that I will break up with you, and you are the last thing I want." She was shouting, and Mike put the phone at some

distance from his ear and nodded like he had had
enough.

"Fine, Holly, I wish you a good day and all the
best to your family," and without listening to more
screaming and cursing, he finished the conversation
and hung up the phone.

Silence. Silence. He looked at his phone, not
happy, and noticed his mother sent him a text to
confirm that they were meeting today.

*Yes, Mum, I will pick you up at 4pm. Looking
forward to seeing you. Love, your precious
son.*

He threw himself on the couch and he fell asleep
immediately. It was so quiet and his house looked
lovely. He felt pleased, as he tidied up yesterday and
he felt he was getting somewhere. He finally was
looking after himself. He did not feel so good for
such a long time and his life was moving somewhere.
Not sure where…

He woke up one hour later and made himself a cup
of tea, and opened a drawer where it was a forgotten
Bible. It was a gift from his mother, probably many
years ago. He picked it up and opened it, and read
in the *New Testament*. He was in *John*. As he was
reading the same question came to his mind: Who are
you, Mike? He felt a thirst to read the Bible and to keep
moving forward, to know more about Jesus.

It was a good question – who are you? And he did
not know who he was. He lost himself in a system

and in a world very complicated. He became something he was not. He was doing things he did not want to do. He was not Mike, no! He changed, but not into something he wanted to be but something he was not. His dreams and passions died and he was just living day by day but not a life filled with joy and love. Just a life.

He felt a pain in his heart and put his hand at his chest. More questions came: Why do you date Holly? She treats you awful! Why do you not speak to Scott, your brother? Why don't you meet him? What do you want in your life? What is your call? Why did you give up on your hobbies? What are your heart's desires?

He picked up his guitar and started playing. He had a few tears coming down on his face and he kept playing. He fell to his knees and put his head down and was crying as a baby. He felt broken, he felt sad, and he felt pain. He did not know who he was. He had a complicated life. The best thing about it was his job as a manager. He took that position last year and was very pleased. That was the only good thing that happened in his life. He liked his job, but that was what he *did*, not who he *was*! Nothing else was good.

His world was falling apart (or maybe parts of it were already broken). He cried for quite a long time and he heard a voice in his heart, the Spirit of the Lord, speaking gently. *I am the way, the truth and the life and I love you*. He took a pillow from the couch and held it tight to his chest and felt so much pain. He realised he was doing so many wrong things and he needed to wake up and find out who he was and start moving in the right direction. He knew he could not do it alone and needed the Lord to help him. Then he felt such a warm feeling of love in his heart and he felt so much love. It was Jesus. Yes, the love of the Lord; *follow me, follow me*, heard in his heart. The Holy Spirit was moving!

He stood up and, having a new strength, he picked up the phone and sent a text message to Holly: *Hi, Holly. I am coming to you at 7pm. Mike*. Then, without not even knowing how, he prayed a very short prayer: "The Lord helped me to find my way and follow you. Help me to find out who I am. In the name of Jesus I pray. Amen."

Chapter 3
Start again

It was 4pm and he picked up his mum (and she was such a lovely lady). She gave him a cuddle and a kiss and always had those soft eyes that brought him comfort. She was so dear to his heart and very fond of his mum. She always offered him love and a warm home, even if he grew up in a way without a father.

"Mum, so nice to see you. You are always so beautiful."

"Thank you, Mike. And you are always such a lovely son."

He helped her get into the car and we both went to a lovely little pub with small wooden tables. It was the Red Bull pub. They used to go there so many times, and it was quiet. All the staff working there knew them, and they kind of had their own table in a way.

"How are you, Mum?" I started the conversation.

"I am fine, son, fine. You know me with my little church and friends." And she looked at him a bit concerned and touched his cheek with her hand.

"You look tired. Is everything all right, my son. How is Holly?"

Mike smiled and took his mum's hand into his and spoke, enthusiastic, "Mum, I went to church today."

His mum, Helena Davis, a lady in her middle 60s, looked a bit shocked at him. Then smiling, said, "The Lord answered my prayers. How did you find it?" She got captivated to hear Mike's story.

"It all started yesterday as I had a lovely dream with an angel that told me to go into a church and walked with me. The angel told me to enter the building as I will find the answers there. So I went to John and his wife. You know John is always with me all the time; is more than a brother. I told John I am going to church and I went with them. It was pretty good. It was a sermon about *The Way, the Truth and Life*."

He seemed so carried away telling her all the stories and how he ended up in the church. His mum was a very good listener.

"That is good, Mike. I am glad you like it. God loves you, and the church is the body of Christ. There are very friendly people and they are there for you to pray and sustain you. And you become part of a family and you are there for them too, like a family."

Mike looked at his mum who was a very patient lady. She was not very tall and dressed very modest in a nice shirt and a cardigan with a dark pair of trousers. She always had the same bag, for years. Was probably what she was fond of.

"In the end, you know, when the service finished, I went in front with many others for prayers and two people prayed for me. After they prayed they had a message from the Lord, a vision: 'who are you, Mike'?"

"True, true. That is good, Mike. You are on the right path!" she encouraged him.

And then with tears coming in his eyes, he said, "I don't really know who I am, Mum. I want to start all things new. I need to start things again, Mum."

His mum touched his face with kindness and said, "Mike, you are a lovely young man. I do want to see you happy and I have not seen you happy in a very long time."

"True, I have not been happy for some years now. It is all a false path and doing wrong things. I believe it is time for me to have a new beginning, Mum."

A waiter came with the food and we changed the subject and talked about funny things. We used to talk about the silly tricks that I did to my mum when I was a child: that I would put salt in the tea or hide and try to scare her. We both laughed. She always told me that I brought her so much joy and I was a lovely son, even if I was cheeky sometimes.

"You had been my son. I could not have asked the Lord for a better one. And you know I am fond of Scott and he was my son, but lived with us for a while."

"You are my only amazingly, beautiful, kind mum!"

"I will be praying for you, son. It will all be fine, do not worry. The Lord is with you and He loves you. He will help you and guide you."

The rest of the evening went by so quickly and we talked about so many things. She told me that Scott, my stepbrother, was doing well. He was my big brother and we just met occasionally at my father's house. She used to speak with him on the phone, and not often visit, but at least he tried some sort of contact.

There was not much connection between us, as he always said he was busy and I did not feel quite accepted. Scott was my father's son, from the first marriage. My parents were divorced for many years. So, when my parents split Scott moved with my father and I remained with my mum; same simple, or complicated, story that was part of my life.

Pete Bolton was the name of my father; was a man who put a lot of emphasis on career, but he himself did not manage much in his life except running a pub with his third wife. Yes, he re-married. However, my mum never re-married. And I felt sad for her as she was a lovely woman. But she always told me she was happy the way she was and she was never alone, that Jesus was with her.

***

It was almost seven o'clock and I kept my word, and I was at Holly's apartment. This time I was ready for going; I was ready to let the Lord do His thing, whatever was, and however He wanted. As soon as I opened the door she looked at me and with big eyes she started talking like the entire world was hers. She did not even say hi or anything, just started telling me about her day and her mum and that it was rude for me not to come. But that was Holly and did not surprise me or made me feel bad this time. She had a tight dress and high heels and she looked ready to go out. She asked me if I wanted a glass of wine.

"No, thank you. You almost finished the bottle, did you, Holly?"

"Yes, and so? It is mine. And you never drink with me. You are so weird. I keep telling you I can find another boyfriend," she shouted at me.

With a very calm attitude, I looked at her. "Actually, Holly, I believe it is time for me to move on. That's why I came! This is not a relationship that works for any of us. So yes, I believe it would be best to break up and find the right person for each other. I am sorry we even dated, but now it is over. Break up and no make up! The end." For some reason I wanted to tell her I am sorry. I felt I was a new man, in a way, or something new was going on inside of my heart and I could not explain it.

Looking around, her house was a mess. In a way she was a nice girl, but not for me. I believe she did not want to change and move on and try better things in her life. I believe she did not want to learn new things. She was plodding along in her life. On the other hand I wanted to move on. I wanted to change and achieve great things in my life. And my life was unhappy, boring and for sure no love. My private love life was boring and I did not feel any love, appreciation, or friendship by being with Holly. She looked at me with big eyes and could not believe it.

"You are serious, Mike, are you? And you even said the words 'I am sorry'."

With a certainty that was not usual for me, and with a courage and a decision that came deep down into my heart, and with the strength and support of the Lord, I spoke boldly. "Yes, I am! I do not think we should have dated in the first place. I am sorry for everything. So let's just move on. I will take the few things I have here and that's it."

She got quiet and looked a bit angry and then she started. "You cannot do this to me. I am Holly, and I did so much for you and you are ungrateful and rude." Here she was starting again her shouting, bragging and hysterical mood, which was well known to me.

"Holly, we broke up so many times. You are always angry and no, I am sorry but this will not work out. I do not love you and you do not love me either. I do not want to be in a relationship that harms both of us. This is best."

At the beginning she seemed to understand and was quiet, then she went into a rage of swearing and kept drinking more wine. I took a little bag with a few books and objects I had around, and in five minutes, with her behind my back screaming, I went toward the door. "Goodbye, Holly. I wish you all the best."

She put her nails into my arm, trying to stop me going and literally scratched me, and I said nothing, but pretty calm, I just walked out. If you would have seen me a few weeks ago, she used to stress me so much and I would have to go into a lecture and be in an encouraging mood as she would go so depressed or screaming. I felt I was a psychiatrist looking after her. She probably needed to find her own way in life, like me. We all have a messed up life and only the Lord can bring us to the shore and light the path and bring us to green pastures with peace, joy and blessings. It is never too late. It is always a new beginning with the Lord, another chance.

I walked toward my car and turned on the engine and pondered for a minute then I said, "Thank you, Jesus, that is a relief. Could not have done that alone!" Driving home I heard my phone ringing but did not answer. Once home I felt so peaceful and like a burden was lifted from my chest.

Immediately, I deleted Holly's phone number as a sign I had moved on. The same time the phone made a noise again and my heart went like a *ping*. Not again! Making faces, I picked up my phone and, for my surprise, it actually was a message from Bella Wilson. She was asking me what time I was going to pick her up tomorrow morning to take her to Westpark Primary School where she was working as a teacher. That was more like it–good message– and replied to her. And then it was *me* time! Finally I had my own time in my own house. I felt I got my life back.

This evening was a beautiful evening. I actually turned on Netflix and managed to watch a good movie. And meanwhile I did a very nice carving. I made a lovely lotus flower. It was carved in wood.

What a day! It seemed from the morning till now, everything changed. My world, which before was upside down, seems to make sense slowly. I had peace in my heart and achieved things that I never planned or even thought would achieve. The Lord and the way the Lord was working was new to me and a surprise, but I was learning to listen to the prompting of the Holy Spirit in my heart.

I was not sure if Holly would still annoy me for the next few days but I was not even concerned about that. I already moved on, and my mind and my heart was moving in another direction of healing, peace, forgiveness and a new journey. Not sure where the road would lead me, but it seemed something new and exciting, and taking a day at a time and following the Lord was the way forward. Who was I? Who is Mike Davis? That was a very good question. It was really deep and I wanted to re-discover myself. I knew it would be a process but I was determined to persevere and go for it.

Later on that evening, I took my guitar and started to put my hand on the strings and felt so good. It was a beautiful evening and I went outside on the porch and admired the stars. I couldn't remember when I did that last time; probably I even forgot how beautiful the stars were – God's creation.

"Thank you, Lord, for whatever you are doing. And help me, as I have no clue what I am doing at the moment and where to go. I need your wisdom and guidance and teach me, spirit, how to follow you," and fell asleep as I kept praying.

The next morning came really quick and it was amazing to get up and see my house clean and nice. I felt it was my home! I dressed with a nice white shirt and put on a pair of black trousers and a lovely brown belt. I was ready to go. Whistling, I looked into the mirror and tidied up my hair and was ready to go. I actually felt confident. I took a blouse but never kind of wore it, and my day started. No thoughts, no worries, just looking forward to seeing more beautiful cars and for a busy day at work.

As I was ready to leave and locked the main door, a car came with speed and parked straight next to mine. For a moment I thought she would hit my car. I was driving a beautiful metallic-blue BMW, a three-years-old baby, and it was very precious to me. It was Holly and I was not happy, but at the same time not concerned and just carried on getting my things in the car. She whooshed out of her car and closed the door of her car with noise and started, like usual, shouting at me.

"You do not answer me when I call you on the phone and then tell me I cannot call you. What is wrong with you?"

I looked at her and with a calm voice I stopped from what I was doing and told her, "Holly, please go and live your life. I told you – no more. It is over. It was over long ago. Please leave. This is my property and my house, and I do not want us to meet again."

She had a cup of coffee in her hand as she was talking to me and out of blue she just threw it in my face. It was not quite the best–unexpected–and my entire white t-shirt ended up stained. Then she got angry, into the car, and shouted as she drove off with speed, "You are nobody, Mike, nobody, and I want to have nothing to do with you anymore."

I did not feel like nobody, I felt like somebody! Me, Mike Davis, living my own life.

I looked at my watch and realised I cannot be late to pick up Bella. I promised to be there at 7.30am. Thinking quickly, I did not have time to change, but I always had extra shirts and clothes in the car, so no problem. I would have to change at work, so took a tissue and wiped my face and looked into the mirror. I laughed. "Not bad, Mike Davis! You still got the looks!"

It was just hitting 7.30am and I finally parked in front of Bella's house and knocked at her door. She opened the door immediately. She looked beautiful. Actually, for a moment I paused and did not know how to react. She had a beautiful dark pink shirt with a nice design and a pair of black trousers. She looked professional.

"Good morning, Bella. I hope I am not late," I apologised.

"No, you are not. Thank you, Mike, for picking me up."

Then, looking at me, she noticed I was all stained with fresh coffee on my shirt. She said nothing, but I noticed her beautiful eyes looking a bit concerned.

"I am sorry. I was splashed with coffee by my ex-girlfriend. Not the way I planned to start my morning. I will have to change at work."

Bella looked at her watch then smiling, added, "I can spare five minutes if you want to use the bathroom upstairs. You can clean up and change. It's all right with me."

For a moment I hesitated and then I said, "Let me go and get a spare shirt from my car, and yes, it would be nice to look a bit better when I go to work." I laughed.

Her house was a small two-bedroom house. Very cosy. As I walked upstairs to the bathroom, I hear her voice behind me at the end of the stairs. "Mike, be careful. Polly, my cat, might be in the bathroom. Just tell her to leave gently, she will be fine. Probably wants a stroke."

"No problem."

In five minutes I was ready and managed to take her to school on time. It was quiet in the car on the road to the school and I decided to ask her a few things. It was quite bold of me as I had not been the best with starting conversations. "Do you go to church for a long time?"

"Actually, I was on and off. I went when I was young, then stopped going for a few years. And being good friends with Emma, I started going again four years ago, after my divorce. But my connection with the Lord was always there, but I did not know how to draw near him."

"I am so sorry to hear that."

"It's all right, the Lord was good to me and healed my broken heart. And now, I am in love with the Lord and just love being at church and with my family of friends there."

We arrived at the school and I parked in front of it. She spoke very gratefully. "Thank you, Mike. And

GRACE TRUE

thank you for sending someone to pick up my car as well. You have been very kind to me and helpful."

For a moment I did not want her to leave. "If you need any other help, I would love to help you, Bella."

She looked shyly and lifted her eyes and our eyes met, then she spoke. "I finish at 4pm and, well, I might be asking too much for a lift back home."

My heart was happy and I was ready to pick her up. "Not at all, not at all. Would be my pleasure. I will send you a message. Sometimes I finish a bit later."

"It's all right, do not worry, Mike. You did quite a lot for me."

Mike insisted and gently touched her hand as she left. "Please, Bella, would be my pleasure. I will send you a text."

As she was leaving, she turned her head and our eyes met again. Looking at my car Bella added, "You have a lovely car!"

Mike drove away happy and smiling, and looking in the rear mirror as he was leaving behind Bella who walked into the main entrance of the school.

Chapter 4
Broken! The lotus flower

The day passed quickly and later on I picked up Bella. I actually enjoyed her company. She seemed like a nice lady and she was 29 years old. Well, a few years younger than me. She had a gentle heart and kind personality and made me feel very relaxed around her. I also felt like she was listening to what I was saying.

A few more days passed and I did not hear from her, and then on Wednesday around 5pm I heard my phone pinging and a message came through and was from her.

Thank you for my car. I got it Tuesday morning. Very kind of you. I will have to sort out the bill. Could I meet you when you are free?

Mike smiled as it was quite unexpected, and sent a short text: *Yes, you can pop round to my house if you want for a cup of tea. I have just got home.* And I gave her my address, waiting to see her reply. She agreed, and 30 minutes later she was knocking at my door. Since I broke up with Holly, it was so quiet in the house and the good part was that she stopped harassing me and chasing me; made me feel that I was starting a new life.

As I was moving around the house to make sure that everything was nice, I started laughing, talking to myself. "Mike, you are getting too carried away as this lady comes by. If she likes you, she will like you for who you are, not your house – hopefully." I started laughing at my thoughts. As I was still doing things, the doorbell rang and took me couple of minutes to answer as felt a bit anxious.

"Hi, Mike!"

"Hi, Bella!" I invited her in and offered her a drink.

"This is yours!" and she handed me my shirt.

Feeling a bit confused, and not sure I knew what it was about. Then I remembered the last goodbye with my ex-girlfriend.

"You forgot it at my house the other day and I just washed and ironed it for you."

Looking at her, I smiled and took it from her, pondering for a minute. "Thank you, Bella. That is very kind of you. Even washed and ironed! I am spoiled."

She looked around and complimented me. "Your house is very nice and tidy and looks lovely."

"Well, I do not have a cat, which I would love. I have a guitar."

She apologised politely. "I won't stay long, maybe you are busy. I just wanted to know how much I need to pay for the car repairs and to give you a cheque." She looked at me, waiting for my answer.

"Bella, you do not need to pay anything as the bill is paid," I added as I invited her to sit down.

She looked at me, surprised. "The bill is paid? How much was it, Mike?"

Looking at her and waiting to see her reaction, I spoke, very relaxed. "Bella, you have been very kind to me and I wanted to show you kindness as well." And I took her hand into mine and held it for a moment.

"You paid the bill?" She looked at me, shy and confused.

"Yes, Bella, I paid the bill. It is paid. You do not need to worry."

We sat down in my lovely little warm conservatory and it was very peaceful. None of us said anything, we were just looking at each other drinking a cold drink.

"So what about you, Mike?" she asked me, looking curious at me, and for a moment I felt a bit embarrassed which was not quite me.

I looked at her and smiled. "You can ask me anything, Bella! I am not a person who has secrets."

She was fiddling with her hair and got shy, then she looked into my eyes and her green eyes had sparkle. "I was wondering about you and your life."

"All right, let me think. I am 35, blue eyes, 1.75cm as you see. Do you think I am handsome? Maybe! Haha," and we both laughed and then I continued on a more serious tone. "I grew up with my mum. My parents have been divorced since I was little. Me and my mum are very close and she goes to a little

Baptist church. I had a bit of a rocky life with few relationships, and for the past year I was on and off with Holly, whom I finally broke up with a few days ago, but the relationship was nonexistent anyway." For a moment I looked down and whispered more for myself then for Bella to hear, "Sadly not really in love, and would like to meet real love one day." Bella was listening and then I kept sharing. "No, I did not have a close relationship with God, but last Sunday I really enjoyed coming to church."

She looked at me and was still listening. I was amazed as she did not interrupt me, not criticise me and did not laugh at me. Not often I would be asked about me–Mike–my life. I carried on with my life story.

"I love carving little figurines and making things out of wood, and playing my guitar. Yes, I love playing when I am free. And yes, a bit of sport, you know. Crazy about swimming when I get a chance." I stood up and behind me on a little table were a few of the figurines covered in a special wood box. And Bella stood up and came near me. She was so close to me and my shoulder touched her hair and I got a bit nervous. She looked at them in amazement, beaming with joy.

"They are wonderful. Amazing, Mike. You are really gifted." I encouraged her to take some if she wanted to look at them.

"Well, it's more like in my free time, a little hobby I have and I love it. I have done it since I was young."

She took the lotus flower and looked at it. "This is beautiful!" and admired it. She was holding it in her both hands and was amazed, looking at the details of the petals.

"I just made it the other day! Do you like it!? Is so precious, isn't it?"

She touched again and looked at it. "So many details, Mike!" She put it down on the table and looked at the others. No one noticed my work before; only my mum loved my figurines. I did not kind of share it and was more like 'me' time and a secret part of my heart undiscovered, private, just me and the Lord.

"Apart from my mum, now you have the honour to see my little collection."

"Really? Thank you, Mike! I appreciate that!" Bella looked at each one of them for quite some time and I kept telling her the story behind each one of my mini carved creations. All of them had a story, a purpose, a reason, and they were in a way special to me.

Looking at the clock she suddenly said, "I believe it is getting late and I would better go home and sort out dinner. And I have some things to do for the school for tomorrow."

"Would you like to stay for dinner?"

Surprised by the invitation, she refused politely. "That is very kind of you. Maybe another time, Mike, thank you."

I felt disappointed and asked again. "Please come for dinner sometimes. I would love to cook for you!"

Bella turned around as she started walking toward the door. "Thank you, Mike."

For a moment I stopped and then a thought crossed my mind and told her, "Wait a minute!" and I rushed back and brought her the lotus flower I carved the other day. "I would like you to have this." She looked at me and was ready to say no. "Please, Bella, don't say no! I want you to have it! *You*, Bella."

She looked at me with her eyes and it seemed to me an eternity and then smiled. "Thank you, Mike, is very kind to you. I will treasure it," and from my hands I put it into hers; from me to her, giving something new, giving something I created; a part of me, a part of my heart, something special and something I wanted only Bella to have. Deep down in my heart was the new beginning, a lotus flower blooming in the season, something made for her, in a way. But the Lord God, the Father, gave much more, gave his son, Jesus. Gave his son for us! Gave us love on a cross! What love!

***

It was Saturday and I went to see John, my friend. I could not believe how quick some days were passing, and for me were days of peace and days of finding myself and finding my way!

"Hi, Mike. How are things?"

And I started to share with him "the Holly story" and that I broke up with her. However, I was more eager to tell him that I managed to fix Bella's car and she popped around for a cup of tea. "Bella seems a very nice lady!"

Emma, who was serving the dinner, spoke up. "That's all, Mike? Nice! Bella is a lovely lady. We have been friends for many years. And she went through a lot. Now she has been alone for so many years."

"I did not know that!" said Mike.

"She is a gentle soul and very caring. She really helped me a lot when I lost my mum. She has a gift for broken hearts. She is a true friend to me." Emma was going into deeper details.

I was silent for a moment and John was quite enthusiastic and spoke up. "Our Mike is growing up. He broke up with Holly!" added her husband.

"Did you, Mike? So now you are single again! You deserve a lovely woman to love you and you to love her!"

Mike looked at them and was not sure what to say. "Yes, I am, and trying to move on with my life. I believe I made a lot of wrong choices in my life. I think I am quite happy by myself for now."

For a moment there was silence again and the subject was changed which I was glad for as probably they noticed I did not feel comfortable to talk about myself and my mistakes or past, and for sure was not in the mood to talk about love.

"Are you coming tomorrow to church?" asked John.

"Yes, I am and I will drive my car. So I won't need a babysitter, John. I am growing up a bit." I said it with a funny voice and made some faces at my friend. John laughed and the day went by unexpectedly as we all enjoyed a lovely meal together. As I was getting ready to leave Emma looked at me.

"Would you like to join us for lunch tomorrow? I invited Bella too."

Mike smiled and looked at her with a shiny face. "I am always eating here! Ha-ha. But for a pretty face like Bella, yes of course I will come. Hope I won't scare her away."

"You will make us all happy and you will always bring joy in this home, Mike! You are like family, you know that, Mike!"

They all laughed and Mike felt so good.

Sunday was a lovely day and Mike enjoyed his time at church. He actually felt like the Lord was speaking to him through the sermons, people, everything around him; was that peaceful voice prompting him inside, and he was listening. Before he left he spoke to a few ladies and they told him all their news about their grandchildren. Mike was a good listener after all (when he was not on his go, go speed). He actually started to like this new path of coming to church on Sunday and making new friends; different than his work.

As he was walking toward the main entrance ready to leave, he saw Bella. She was coming from kids groups and she smiled and he waved at her. His heart was filled with joy. She really looked so beautiful.

It was lunchtime and we both were at Taylor's house at 1pm. As I parked the car, Bella drove in and parked hers next to mine. I went near her car and, polite, I opened her car door and she looked at me.

"Hi, Mike. Thank you. How are you?"

"I am fine, thank you, Bella."

We both walked together and she stopped and turned toward me. "I really need to thank you again for the lotus flower. It is so special and beautiful. I really appreciate it. Thank you, Mike."

"I think I was meant to carve it for you. You are very special and beautiful, Bella."

Before she could answer, our conversation was interrupted by John who welcomed us. Emma already was in the kitchen and Bella went to help her with the sandwiches and lunch. In no time we were all in the lounge and were enjoying a nice small lunch with a variety of sandwiches and a comfortable chat, relaxed. Emma's phone rang and she apologised and left the room.

"How was the kids group at church today, Bella?"

"It was lovely. I was with 4–5 years old and were adorable. They even said a few prayers. Is amazing what children can pray for. So sweet and truthful and make prayers so simple, and we adults always complicate and find it hard to open our hearts and speak the truth as children do."

"Yes, they are lovely. They just speak what is on their heart," John agreed.

"Are you helping with the kids, Bella?" asked Mike.

"Yes, twice a month, and I love it. It is so rewarding to serve and help others, and especially children. They make you smile and love you unconditionally."

Emma entered the lounge and said to John, her husband, and to the other guests, "John, my dad called. I have to go and help him with shopping. So sorry, Mike, Bella. I will leave you with John. I need to help my father, otherwise he won't manage to finish shopping in two hours. He moves so slow with his arthritis. See you maybe later. If not, catch up soon. 'Bye."

John followed her and you could hear voices in the distance as she was ready to leave out the door. It was late 3pm and Mike felt tired.

"I am going to leave soon, I feel a bit tired now."

"Me too," said Bella. "I am meeting my mother this afternoon."

We both left the same time and as I was saying goodbye to Bella, next to my gorgeous car, I asked her, "So, Bella, when are you going to accept my invitation for dinner?"

Bella looked at me and, thinking, she said, "What about next Saturday?"

That made me quite happy, and getting courage I continued. "Great. Can I cook for you? Would you like to come to my house or go out?"

She smiled and nodded the same time as she spoke. "Looking forward to seeing what you are going to cook for me, Mike."

"Will be a surprise. Shall we say 4pm?"

"Great, see you then."

As I left home I felt quite happy. I was going to cook for a very nice lady. Bella was nice and patient and kind. And the only other person I enjoyed cooking for was for my mother.

Home. I sat down and played my guitar. I really loved playing it and it was music to my heart. Suddenly the words 'I am sorry' came to my mind. I had been thinking of those words for some time. I felt in my heart that I had to settle some things with some people and that I might have been judging them or not treating them quite fairly. Even if I was told by my mother that I did nothing wrong, I still did not feel I had a right relationship with my father or Scott. Actually, I had none at all. Out of blue, I decided to call John.

"Hi, Mike. Is everything all right with you? You just left our house an hour ago."

"John, I want to get baptised!"

John got really shocked and explained a few things to me. But to me it was something I felt I needed to do. I needed Jesus and I had been discovering a different kind of world – the world of love, where there was a great saviour who died for me, and His love was amazing. It was something for my heart, for me. When I spoke with my mum on the phone she was really encouraged. I was on a new path with the Lord and listening to his spirit and yes, I wanted to get baptised.

***

So this coming Saturday I went to church. It was a small group: me, Bella, John, Emma and my mum. We had George and Maria Lewis, the main leaders of the church, and a few other members like Peter Williams, Sarah Baker–part of the church family– and only a few others. It was a small group for my baptism and it made me feel quite good, and I was ready. However, George Lewis did have a conversation with me earlier in the week and asked me questions regarding why I was doing it and how much I knew about Jesus. Well, I wanted to do it so I can have a fresh new relationship with Jesus and start my new road, my walk with the Lord, life with Jesus and Heaven. How much I knew was not much. I was a bit lost in space and did know mostly the *New Testament*, about Jesus's life, but never read the Bible step by step. It was quite something new for me and was at the beginning of the walk with Jesus.

It was not an impulsive decision. It was something that I had been thinking for years, then put back in my heart and mind and then it surfaced again and again. Yes, my heart was desiring a relationship with the Lord and wisdom, guidance, grace, peace, joy and all the good things mentioned in the Bible.

They took a lot of pictures at my baptism and it would be shared on Sunday at church and I would be introduced to the church family. I did not want to do it Sunday as it was too much for me and was too overwhelming in front of the entire church.

Later on the same day Bella came to my house. As I opened the door, she brought me a wrapped gift and that surprised me as usually my mum would remember my birthday. But it was not my birthday and I could not remember the last time I received a gift. Probably at Christmas from John and Emma. I was in the middle of cooking with an apron and dressed nicely with a blue t-shirt, and the table was already prepared.

"Hi, Mike. This is for you." She handed me the gift.

That was so thoughtful of her. That touched my heart and she noticed my shy smile and my clumsy gestures when I took the gift from her hands. "Hi, Bella. Come in, come in. Thank you. That is very sweet of you. I don't remember the last time I got a gift."

"So, what are you cooking for me?"

"Something Italian. Hope you will like it!"

She came into the kitchen and noticed all looked nice. "This is very nice. I feel spoiled."

I looked at her and invited her to sit down. "You look beautiful, Bella. This is only something I organised. I am sure you deserve much more than that."

She got shy and our eyes met and she smiled at me. "Thank you, Mike!"

Then, looking curious, I asked her if I can open the gift.

"Of course, you can. Is for you." She looked excited to see if I would like it.

As I opened it, my hands started to shake a bit as I was emotional. She came near me and touched my hands and I turned and looked at her.

"Hope you will like it. It is special for you, Mike!"

It was a box with a lot of compartments. And then I saw it was a small tool set I could use for my carving. It was lovely. I stood up and came near her and did not know what to do and how to react and how to say thank you. "Thank you," and I kissed her quickly on the cheek, avoiding her eyes, and gave her a hug.

She looked at me, surprised, and her green eyes were shining. "Welcome to the Kingdom, Mike!"

I laughed and felt so happy. "Yes, there are a lot of things happening around me and some do not make sense. But I love every bit of it. It feels like my life has some sort of sparkle now, when before it was quite boring."

We sat down for dinner in my small kitchen and we spoke about a lot of things and we laughed together. It felt good to meet her again and spend time with her. In some things we were the same and in others so different. We stopped for a moment and we looked at each other. She smiled and then said that she would have to leave soon. I wished she would have stayed longer but I was happy even to spend a few hours with her, and the fact that she accepted my invitation for dinner. It was a beautiful night, a night to remember, and a friendship that was slowly growing.

Chapter 5
"I am sorry!" list

Next day came quickly and then the days passed quickly as well. And in my heart it started to get birthed with interesting things. As much as I was praying and talking to the Lord, listening; as much as I wanted things to change in my family, funny enough but serious, I made a list and I called it "I am sorry!" list.

It was a list on which I put all the names of some people that I especially prayed for and I wanted to get in contact with. From colleagues to my father's side of the family; was kind of a very interesting list. A desire to say I am sorry and try maybe to reconnect with them, started to bring re-birth in my heart.

The top of that list was my father, Pete, and Scott. That was the hardest. Actually, there were a few others I wanted to say I am sorry to, (were some of my colleagues). But that was all. My main big "I am sorry" was Scott and my father.

John advised me for the past few days to forgive, to forgive and let go of the past, and gave me a few scriptures as I shared with him about my list. It was a long process to forgive. I would sit sometimes in the evening and be there, but my heart was not there and my mind either. Forgiveness was not easy for me. It was a slow and painful process and I was not sure even what I was doing.

Many times we put things back in our mind, lock them in our heart, put them aside and do not deal with them or avoid them and hope it will pass. But the pain does not go away, is still there, and does not help us move forward. It is something like a wall that blocks us and pops around, and we do not know why we react in certain ways. It is because we are burdened with sorrow and sadness and pain, and we need to surrender to the Lord, forgive and let go. How will I move on?

At work I managed just to have a little chat with my colleagues over lunch and apologise for the past and they were actually surprised. Few of them did not even remember what it was about. Probably some sort of misunderstanding regarding a car or a client: "Is something I felt I had to do since I sorted things out in my life. So, I am taking one thing at a time as I start a new life with Jesus. Might not make sense for you, but this is what my heart tells me to do."

"No problem, is actually very kind of you. I even forgot about it. Nothing to worry about, but very much appreciated–your attitude–and thank you," I was told by a colleague.

Sunday came and I went to church, and managed to get a glimpse of Bella. Did not plan it, but she seemed to be here and there and everywhere.

John, looking at me and the way I reacted, spoke up. "Why don't you go and speak with her, Mike?"

Mike looked at him and smiled, sad. "I would like that. She seems really great, but I am not ready, not yet. I have lots of things that my heart needs to deal with and I'm not really ready for a girl like her. She might be even too much right now!"

My friend tap me on a shoulder with compassion. "That's sad. She is such a lovely lady. And is not dating anyone at the moment, actually for years since she broke up."

Mike looked at his friend. "I think I get the idea, John, but I am not ready. My heart needs sorting out first. And that is quite a journey for me. Very much a challenge."

John added, as he was ready to leave, "Well, just don't take too long. By the time you wake up, she might not be here anymore. And our heart always needs Jesus. You will always have to deal with a lot of things. Don't delay it too much, Mike."

Mike looked at her, and Bella noticed him and waved. He smiled and he got the idea of his friend and he was actually right. With him and her it was not quite the right timing for now. Well, he was at the beginning of the journey with Jesus and he was quite on a different road than her, trying to sort out the pain from the past. He felt sad in his heart that he really liked her and after such a long time he finally believed that he met an amazing lady and Bella was quite a lovely woman. And he really enjoyed her company.

But for him to move on, he would have to sort out some things and he would have to deal first with some things from his past. And he did want to try things with his father and Scott. They might never accept him or love him, but he wanted to say I am sorry and meet them and be there for both of them. He was not even sure why he was sorry. Well, he wanted to try but was not sure how he would do it. Once he would do that, he might think of Bella. His heart needed a lot of healing after Holly and the past, and he needed to know clearly before jumping again into a relationship.

As he got home he looked at his phone three times and finally dialled his father's phone number. Pete picked up the phone and his voice was just polite and indifferent.

"Hello, Dad, this is Mike."

"Hello, Mike, how are you?"

"I am fine, thank you, Dad. I am fine. How are you?"

My heart started to beat up really quick, and was not sure at that moment that it was quite a good idea to speak with him. He would always give me a lecture and tell me how great Scott is and then kept talking and I would feel that I never matter, and in the end, after 40 minutes of listening, I would hang up the phone and I would feel bad. But this time I was determined to do a good job, but was not sure how to do it. But that's why I had the Holy Spirit; he knew better than me how to guide me. God's wisdom would help me and teach me how to speak and be patient enough with my father, and probably with myself.

"I am fine, busy, you know. Very busy. But I was thinking of giving you a call so we can have a chat." And he went on and kept telling me all his problems in the past week and I knew it would take a long time, and it did. It was literally 40 minutes so I just sat down on the couch and relaxed.

In the end, my father seemed so happy and actually I felt pretty good that I listened to him and he even invited me over.

"Why don't you come next week on Saturday? We are having a barbeque and it will be great. It will be of course Scott here, and I am sure he will bring his girlfriend. Or maybe he broke up. I can't remember." My father laughed. "Anyway, we will be here and will have all the fun. I invited, you know, my old friends. So just maybe 10 of us. What do you say, Mike?"

"Yes, Dad, thank you. Yes. It would be good to see you and Scott. All the best to Molly, and take care."

The Lord seemed to open a new door for me, however I was not sure. I still felt new in all this journey and some things were totally out of my control, but I did want to be a better son and try to reconnect with my father and for sure with Scott, my stepbrother. Each time I tried with Scott he would push me aside with the reason that he was busy. And at that time I did not really make an effort. My relationship with my father was just plodding along and with my brother was basically, from my point of view, nonexistent.

The next few days went pretty quick for me as I was focused about meeting my father. My prayers were like a healing road for me and I was really determined to clean up my life slowly with the help of the Holy Spirit.

I had been thinking in my quiet moments of carving or playing my guitar, that I would have liked to invite Bella again for dinner but I was not ready. No, my mind was all over the place and my heart had so many wounds and for sure I was not ready for a relationship. And seeing her would make me want to see her more and more, and she was so different from other ladies. Maybe I was afraid to fall in love as she was so special and she was "Bella". Not sure I wanted the path of another relationship yet.

Saturday was here and I was knocking at my father's door and Molly, his wife, opened the door. She was a short lady, very kind, giggling a lot, and I gave her a bouquet of flowers. She gave me a hug. She never had children of her own but she was always nice to me and Scott. My father came by and I gave him a bottle of wine.

"Mike!" He came near me and I actually gave him a hug and he was so surprised.

"Hello, Dad! So nice to see you and Molly. Thank you for the invite."

People slowly started to come in and I offered to help Molly with the cooking. Well, there was not much to do but I just enjoyed a little chat with Molly. She was the chattiest in the family. Scott, like usual, would show up the last 30 minutes or so as he was always busy. And he was not much with parties, but he always showed our father and the stepmom respect.

"Lovely weather today. I was afraid it would rain."

"No, it is actually good, isn't it?"

My father looked at me and seemed a bit like studying me and he took me aside and talked, very private. "Mike, you do look different. So, what's going on in your life?"

"Dad, I broke up with Holly. I was promoted. Maybe you remember, it happened last year, and I am really enjoying my job. And I turned to God and became Christian some time ago. Yes, things are different. Still enjoying my friendship with John and making lots of new friends."

My father, who was not very tall, looked at me, surprised, but pleased in a way. I did share all of those in just a few seconds and did not want to enter in details – at least not today.

"Good for you, Mike. Good for you."

Looking at my father I smiled and said, very direct, "Dad, it has been on my heart that maybe I was not such a great son to you and I did not visit as much as I should, or call you. So, I would like to say I am sorry and would like to reconnect with you, when you have time. If you are busy, I understand. I just want you to know that I am here too for you." It was not easy for me to say it but I felt really happy and at peace that I did. I was showing grace.

His father looked, so touched, at me and had a few tears in his eyes and gave me a tight hug and said, "Thank you, Mike. That means quite a lot for me. I would love that." As Mike was getting back to the kitchen to help Molly, his father called him back. "Mike, actually it is not your fault. I know you went through a lot as a child. And I am sorry. I wished I would have been a better dad." And he gave him another hug and left quickly to talk to his friends, probably being a bit embarrassed.

Mike felt touched and felt that he went a step forward in his decision to reconcile with his other side of the family. His mother was not having much contact with his father, just occasionally, more like once a year a merry Christmas message, and rarely phone calls.

Just before the party was over, Scott showed up and he walked straight in. He was not the most popular or the one to enjoy parties. But I can tell you one thing about him: he was a brilliant doctor. He was one of the best. All in one! And he loved his job.

"Hey, Dad, Molly!" and gave them a hug. He then took some food and spoke to other people. I kept trying to find a moment to talk to him, but did not. So I decided to finally approach him without preparing my mind and heart and not thinking if I would do the right or the wrong thing.

"Hey, Scott, how are you?"

He looked at me with indifference and he was tired and bored. "Hey, Mike, fine, thank you. Just broke up with my girlfriend." He laughed.

Then I said too, "I broke up with mine too. Ha-ha, good synchronisation."

"What are you up to, Mike?" (Pretended to care.)

"Not much, not much, just usual work."

"Yes, yes, you should come to my hospital and see how busy we are. We had a breakthrough this week and managed to look after a 25-year-young man and we did an amazing surgery. Fantastic!"

"You really love your job, Scott, and it seems much more to you. I am sure you are doing a good job."

My father came near and spoke up to defend his first-born from the first marriage. He did that many times and was so proud of Scott. "He is brilliant! The best cardiologist!"

"Dad, you do not need to lift me up in the skies!" Scott felt a bit embarrassed, which was not of him.

As my father was saying goodbye to some of his friends, I decided to be bolder. "Scott, I just wanted to apologise to you and say I am sorry, that I did not spend too much time with you and didn't, you know… call you."

Scott looked at me funny and, sarcastic, said, "Come on, Mike, we are not kids anymore!"

"No, but I wished I would have been a better brother for you and be there for you, and maybe catch up sometimes."

Scott had a total different approach than my father. "Yeah, yeah. Nice of you. But I am very busy, you know. Working in a hospital is not like working in an office. It is a responsibility, Mike!" and he went into one of his moods, telling me how wonderful his job was and carried on for 30 minutes till everyone left.

Amazingly I listened to him, not being anxious but trying to get more and more into his world and to understand him. But only the Lord would probably know the heart of my brother. Then he apologised and just left out of the blue and I was alone with my father and Molly. And then it was my time to leave. Something actually changed. Even if Scott did not have a positive attitude, my father did, and I felt his heart changed and his behaviour toward me, and for the first time in a long time I gained some respect from my father which I never had before. I was hoping it would last and was not something passing by or for the moment. But only trusting in Jesus–that was helping me–and knew my heart in this matter.

Tomorrow was Sunday so I went to bed early as I felt too tired as this was something I never have done before, to say I am sorry to my father and Scott. However, I managed to share with Mum that I had a touching chat with my father, which she was really happy with – that I am trying to connect again with him.

Chapter 6
How long will it hurt?

Today was Sunday and I was so glad to go to church, but deep down in my heart I felt a pain and was not sure what it was. I managed to listen to the service but my chest was filled with pain and it was not easy for me; a deep pain, and it hurt; was something emotional and not really physical, maybe anxiety. I could not tell.

As I was leaving, I just said a few hellos to a few of the people and was not in the mood for deep conversations this time and to stick around. As I went into my car I felt I would crash emotionally and would not be able to hold myself on till home. I was parked far away so was sure that no one would notice me. I rested my head on the wheel and felt like crying. I stayed like this in quietness and then I heard a knock at my car window, and it was Bella. She was the last person in the world that I wished to see. I opened the window, and very kindly she asked me:

"Hi, Mike, are you all right?"

I did not know what to say, but was not in the mood for anybody, and with a cold voice, not very polite, I said firmly, "I just want to be left alone, Bella. Is it too much to ask?"

Bella, very polite, backed down and apologised. "I am so sorry to have disturbed you, please forgive me. Just wondering how are you as I have not heard from you in a long time. Take care and God bless." And she said all those so quickly and turned around, left immediately.

I then drove off, not very happy, and felt angry with myself. I was not sure why and what was going on but felt a lot of pain, and even at home could not eat or do anything and decided to sit at God's feet and ask and listen and find out what it was about.

Then the Lord kept bringing to my heart and in my mind a picture of Scott. Yes, it was actually about Scott. I wanted so much and for so long to reconcile with my brother, but in a way I did not need that. We did not have an argument. The only thing was, it was the fact he was my stepbrother and he was always living with my father. He lived with me for just few years and then when my parents split he went to live with my father. He chose, so as he was his son and elder.

I never felt accepted by my brother and never felt loved by him for sure, or even liked. That hurt me. And even when being young, I kept trying to do my best and it never was good enough. Anything I tried, it seemed that Scott never wanted to have much to do with me and for sure did not want me as a brother or even to be friends with me at all.

I felt it was my fault, and that was painful. I did my best and, well, he did not really accept or believe my apologies, and for sure did not change his behaviour toward me and went to the same tune for years.

Then I felt as bad as I whooshed Bella, and she was kind and polite to me. And I did not have quite a nice attitude with her. It was true we did not communicate for some time but maybe because my focus was somewhere else, trying to fix the past instead of letting God deal with it in His own way. I picked up my phone and dropped her a message.

Hey, Bella, How are you? Look, about today, I had been in a bad mood. So sorry for not being polite with you.

Then I thought for a moment and spoke to myself. "I will try!" then carried on typing the message.

Please accept my invitation for dinner as an apology. You name the day and hour. Mike.

It passed quite some time, maybe one–two hours, and very late, 10ish. I received a message.

Hi, Mike, very nice to hear from you. I got the idea today you were not feeling very well. Maybe another time, Mike. Thank you. Praying for you. Have a blessed week. Bella.

It felt like a big bang that sent a message into my heart. Well, she shut me out, or maybe I was more sensitive than usual. I really wanted to say apologies. She had been so nice to me. I still had a heart full of pain and trying to sort out some of my mess, and it felt quite a challenging road for me. It was so painful sometimes, but basically I got the idea that the Lord was healing me and cleaning me and shaping me, and helping me to move forward. I was getting stronger, wiser and also more filled with joy and peace, even if I had days or hours when it felt like I was going backward. I was not, I was moving forward, and even John and Emma, and my mother, and the people from my work told me I changed. I was not sure I did change, or how, but, well, that was good; moving forward slowly.

I was learning to trust in the Lord and give him my past and pain, and let go of the past. I was learning to surrender every part of my life, my thoughts, my heart – me, Mike!

The week passed, and I had to say quite a lot of prayers for both Scott and Bella. It was a bit of contradictions or confusion in my heart (or I was not sure what I was doing). I really wished so much I would have met Scott and for him to try to make an effort. Sadly, as much as I hoped for my father to make an effort, he did not and I found myself sending a message and waiting for three days for an answer. My mum did tell me to take it easy and not to get carried away. And, well, it was not the best; waiting and trusting that the Lord was working. Surrendering was hard.

Sunday was more than welcomed for me as I had been enjoying my new friends at church, and was great. I would go early for a chat and even stay late and try to help and get involved more. John and Emma were always, there helping and serving. As I was ready to leave, I just saw Bella. I did not know today she was not serving with the kids and I wanted so much to speak to her, but she was on the other side of the church and so many people, and few people started to talk to me and I got lost into the group. A young lady with beautiful brown eyes approached me and said hello.

"Hello, I am Martha. Emma told me you are working at a company with cars, and could help me buy myself a new car."

I looked at her, surprised, and for a moment I lost my focus from Bella and looked at this young lady who was smiling and trying to get my attention. "Hello, Martha. Yes, I am Mike and yes, I could probably help you to buy a car. Depends what are you looking for."

She was a nice lady with dark hair and seemed very chatty. That moment Emma came near me and spoke up. "Good, you met my friend, Martha. She works at the library and she is a lovely lady. She wants to buy a new car and I told her I just know the man for it. Our lovely good friend, Mike."

"Yes, Emma. Thank you." My mind raced in all directions and then suddenly realised that Bella probably left the building. And I really wanted to speak with her. I took a visit card from my pocket and gave it to Martha and told her if she is interested in buying a car to give me a call. As I left the building, I felt a bit sad and I really wanted to speak to Bella.

My mum called me later on and wanted to meet me so much and said she needs to speak with me.

"Mum, would you mind coming to my house? I just want to stay home today."

"All right, Mike. I will cook something and bring it over for dinner. What do you say? So like this we will have time for a chat."

"That would be great, Mum, thank you."

As it was 4pm, the usual time for my mum and me to meet on Sunday, she knocked at my door with a big casserole. "Hey, Mike, you look good; a bit tired!" and she gave me a hug.

I leaned and gave her a hug, and invited her in. It was a quiet afternoon for me, and Mum tried so hard to make conversation.

"Mum, I am struggling lately!" I spoke up.

"Yes, Mike, I know you are. I know."

"You know, I tried my best with Dad and even said I am sorry. And was so encouraged that maybe we will have some sort of relationship, and things are actually not changing. And Scott? Nothing, he just does not want to know about me."

Mum looked at me and touched my face with her hand. She had compassion for me and she did understand me as she went through quite a lot with Dad.

THE TEST OF LOVE: BROTHERS FOR LIFE

"Mike, healing is a process and takes time. I believe you are hurting and it is not easy for you. Have hope, and let the Lord lead you and guide you. Mike, not all the time you can reconcile or get back into some relationships. You see, it took me years and years to forgive your father. It hurt me so much. Mike, I tried so hard and then one day the Lord finally made a breakthrough into my heart and got it. I was not responsible for your father or anyone else. I was responsible for myself. And I did my part with your stepbrother, Scott, as well. I accepted it even if it hurt me, and I forgave your father. I gave the matter fully, fully, Mike, to the Lord. I surrendered and did not try anymore. I let the Lord carry me through. Do you understand this son?"

"I will have to think of all those, Mum, and yes, you are right, it is painful."

The rest of the evening went pretty well and we enjoyed a lovely time talking about all kinds of things.

"You started to change, Mike, and is good, but learn to walk bold and confident. God is with you and he will not leave you. You are one of his children now and he is making a way in your heart and life. Trust the Lord and let him lead you."

***

A few more weeks passed like this, and John and Emma decided to start a small house group. I decided to be part of it and it was good as I met lots of people my age. It was Emma, and John, and Martha, and a few others. I liked Rachel and Mark, and an elderly couple. And it was weekly in the evening from 7pm to 8pm. For me, it was pretty good timing.

The first couple of weeks were great and I loved it, and made good friends and enjoyed speaking with Mark, and Rachel, and Martha. It was good to make more friends. And since I started this new path of walking with the Lord it passed a few months, and yes, my mum and even John and my colleagues told me I started to change, which was in a way good. But mostly I was moving on with my life, and it felt that way.

It was a Tuesday evening as I walked in at John's house. Everyone was there, and me (as usual Tuesday working late) I was always getting on time or 5–10 minutes late. But it was nice to have very understanding friends. As I wanted to sit down, I just notice Bella sitting on one of the couches and my eyes got big. Emma spoke up, smiling:

"You know Bella, Mike. She joined the group last week and we already welcomed her. So it is good to have another friend with us."

That Tuesday I felt a bit different. No, I did not forget about Bella, but thinking so much of my father, Scott, the past and trying to understand what the Lord was doing, she was more on standby mode. And since she refused or pushed aside my last invitation, I lost courage.

She was somewhere in my heart, and I was waiting and waiting.

We had a lovely Tuesday with good conversation from the Bible. John would do a great job leading a small discussion based on scripture, and then Emma was doing the prayers and asking if we wanted to share something and pray for something. It was very good and encouraging for me.

Usually I would be the last one leaving on Tuesday and enjoyed a few minutes catching up with John at the door. As I was leaving, John smiled at me and I asked him, as he gave me a long look, "What are you thinking, John?"

"Nothing much, Mike!" and he smiled.

Looking at him, I was really curious, and wanted to know what the idea was this time.

"I was thinking of you. You were funny today!"

"Funny?" I smiled.

"You need to do something about Bella!"

"Do something? What do you mean?" I felt confused.

"It is obvious you like her and it would be nice for you to make up your mind with her, or regarding her."

"Make up my mind?"

"Yes, Mike. What planet are you on?"

Looking down, all kinds of feelings invaded my heart and my mind, and I spoke, very discouraged. "John, she is quite adorable. However, my heart has a lot of things to deal with and at this point in time, not sure I would know what to do with a beautiful angel like Bella. I did not even think of it. Probably I would fail, as usually I am not good with relationships. You should know that pretty well as you walked with me as a friend on this road a few times."

John put his hand on my shoulder and looked at me. "You are a very good friend and a very nice man. I believe you should make time for Bella in your life and try to figure out your heart before it might be too late. You know, you are not the only man in the church, and in the world. I keep telling you that." He laughed.

As I left, I tried to think but could not and dismissed Bella, then sent her a message and tried again.

Hey, Bella, it was so nice to see you tonight. You know the dinner invitation is still open. Mike.

Hey, Mike, it was nice to see you as well. Yes, I know it's still open. Thank you. Bella.

***

One more week passed and it was September, and I felt the summer was gone so quickly.

Bella spent some time at John's house with Emma and had a lovely time chatting. Sometimes they would gather together and plan some things for the church or kids groups. They loved organising things for Christmas and they were part of the gift team.

"I was thinking, Bella, what do you think about our Tuesday group?"

"It is very good and all of us are really connecting well, and I love the Bible discussions and prayers."

Out of the blue, Emma spoke, very direct. "Good. And what do you think of Mike?"

Bella laughed and looked at her friend. "Mike?" A bit surprised and feeling invaded of feelings, she was not sure how to react.

"Yes. What do you think about him?"

"He seems like a nice person. He looked after my car a few months ago and invited me for dinner once. And that is all."

"That is all?"

Bella looked down and fiddled a bit with the pen in her hand then lifted her eyes up and said to Emma, "Well, Mike is a very kind man, very patient. Actually, he keeps inviting me every couple of weeks for dinner."

"And?" Emma was curious.

"And I did not accept another invitation!"

Emma looked at her and made a face. "Why not, Bella? He is a very nice man. We have been friends with him for so many years. John has been very good friends with Mike, and he is quite a kind man. And he has such a good heart; handsome, good job."

"I felt he was not ready for me, and maybe I was not ready for him, you know, maybe to move things forward."

"Is this true?"

"No. I really did not know what to do. Though the best for me is to stay in my situation and plod along. Challenges in a relationship would be quite a lot for me."

"Well, did you think maybe to accept the invitation, or it might not be available next time. Also maybe you hurt him?"

"Yes and no. Maybe I am afraid to be around him as I like him too much." Bella got red.

Emma laughed as John entered the dining room.

"Am I missing something?"

"I am trying to convince Bella to accept Mike's dinner invitation!"

"Good, she is as stubborn as Mike. Great.! Prayers, Emma dear, prayers! God can move these two – we can't." He laughed and looked at his wife. Then, as he wanted to leave, he turned around and said. "I have an idea. Look, Bella, I have some books I need to give to Mike and, well, tomorrow is Saturday. Maybe you can drop them for me?"

Bella looked at him. "Come on, John, really?"

"Really," both of them laughed. "We need to get you two moving somehow. Now you have a reason to go."

She took the books, and as she was leaving said, embarrassed, "I cannot believe I am doing this!"

Later on in the evening Mike already dropped her a message as she was home:

Hi, Bella. John sent me a message that you might be dropping some books for me tomorrow as he is busy.

Bella decided to give him a chance.

Hi Mike. Yes, I wanted to send you a message to find out what time is best for you? But I could stay for lunch, if it's fine with you, and still the open invitation?

That was quite unexpected for me but very welcomed. Probably I gave up asking her for lunch as I always got a no.

Lunch on me. And a walk?

It was quiet for one hour and I gave up, decided to go to bed and maybe tomorrow will be a better day. She was coming, after all. However, my heart felt filled with emotions and was really looking forward to seeing her and spending some time with her. The only time when I had a chance to see Bella lately was at church and at Tuesday group. But no, otherwise I did not have a chance with her alone since she saw my little collection of carved objects. From my part it was a good day that she finally was coming over, and was at the right time. The Lord orchestrated everything so well, and I did have peace about meeting her, and was ready for it.

Chapter 7
One step back or one step forward

It was a beautiful day of September and I was looking forward to meeting Bella, and when I looked at my phone I jumped off the couch. I definitely had to move otherwise she would find me in bed. But that was not me, but I still wanted the house to look good for Bella–extra touch– which my mum would probably say that I exaggerate.

It was 9am and I was having my morning tea and was watching the news. And the message from Bella was a yes, and she said yes she would love to come for lunch and for a walk. For a moment I was not sure what I was doing for lunch and not sure about the walk. I had to read three times the message to make sure I got it, and was so happy and jumped around. "Thank you, Lord, thank you. I can't believe it."

Maybe I was ready to stretch and go further and further, and after a few months since I broke up with Holly, my heart was healed. Was it healed? Some people told me they were not healed for years. Well, the Lord did heal me, and each heart and circumstance is different.

As I moved around as quickly throughout the house, trying to make things nice for Bella, soon it was 11am and I realised she will be here around 12pm. I went into the shower, and dressed nice with a t-shirt and a pair of blue jeans. I looked in the mirror for the first time in ten years and smiled sadly. The years passed and I was not in my 20s anymore, and I was in my middle 30s, and the time flew away. However, today in my life I felt something good was about to come. And today was Bella.

It was 12pm and I was ready, looking at my watch and waiting. As soon as I heard the doorbell I was flying there.

"Hi, Mike!" She smiled and looked at me and brought me the books. She also had a book. She gave it to me. "Those are from John but this one is one of my favourites. You can read it – it's from me: *Make music to my heart* by Grace True. See, you might like it! I enjoyed it."

Mike asked her to sit down and then very politely spoke to her. "What would you like, Bella? I can organise sandwiches here and then go for a walk, or go for a walk and eat out."

She looked at him, surprised by his soft voice, probably not meeting him in a long time, forgetting that Mike was a very polite, kind man. "Mike, would it be fine to actually go for a walk and have something to eat when we come back? Is that all right with you?"

"That will be good with me, no problem."

We started walking and the park was like a 30-minute walk from me, and then we strolled along the park. The conversation at the beginning was basic and felt a bit boring, but I was not the best at starting a conversation.

"Do you have brothers, Mike? Family? I think you mentioned it to me, but could not remember, really."

"Yes, I do have a stepbrother, Scott. And he is my father's son from the first marriage. I had been living with my mum (Helena is her name) for many years. My parents have been divorced since I was young and my stepbrother moved with my father. He is re-married now, with Molly. Probably have told you those things before, but it is complicated when you have so many relatives."

Bella was listening, very patient, and then she added, "Must have been challenging and hard for you and your mum, and I am sure it was not easy for your father too."

Mike turned his head and stopped as they were walking. "Actually, my mum always had a strong faith. The Lord is good. Even when I was a child, I remember her praying for us and praying for things and around the house. I am very close to her and love her dearly."

Bella asked, more boldly, "Are you keeping in touch with your father?"

"Yes, always did, but not as much as I wished I would have. I am trying to reconnect better with my father and his family, and Scott. I am doing my part and it is up to the Lord." Then, looking at her, I wanted to know more about her. It had been fascinating to be with her and she had been so patient with me; no one asked me about my family before, or even wanted to know about me and my passions and dreams, hobbies, life. "How about you?"

"Well, my life is a bit simpler than yours, Mike, or maybe I think that way. I was raised by my mother too as I lost my father when I was young. Was a car crash. And I am also close to my mum. But a few years ago I ended up in a wrong relationship and was married two years, and went through a rough divorce. And now is just me and my cat and the Lord. I am so grateful."

"Did you ever think that maybe you could meet someone else?" I asked, and Bella made big eyes and did not really know what to answer.

A few ladies with children passed by and smiled at us, and we kept walking. You could hear the wind in the trees whispering and it was a beautiful day. The sun was playing hide and seek behind the clouds but it was a warm day in September and no sign of rain.

"After being in a coercive marriage, not sure. I went through a painful stage of healing and forgiveness, and was a journey of a few years that the Lord had to carry me through. And then I met Emma, and she was very supportive as well – both her and John. And now it seems peaceful in my life.

Not sure. I do not want to end up again with the wrong guy, but at the same time, I did not think at all about it. Probably is the last on my prayers list to pray for a partner. Trust is not easy if you are broken, Mike!"

"Yes, I know, it took my mum many years to forgive and move on after my father divorced!"

The rest of our walk we talked about all kinds of things as Bella and I both loved nature. I kept trying to convince her to change her car but without success. We walked back home and it was 1.30pm, and I felt hungry. "I am so hungry, maybe we walked too much!" I felt like eating half of the refrigerator.

"I am fine, I do not usually eat much for lunch."

We walked in and I asked her, "Would you like me to organise a selection of sandwiches?"

"Just one sandwich for me with salad and some ham and maybe a tomato."

"That's all?" I was surprised.

We had a lovely lunch and we sat quiet at my small dining table. We then went to my conservatory where I had a set of very nice couches and was very warm all the time. We had a drink and we chilled out. She looked at me and looked at her watch.

"It is almost 2.40pm and is getting late, so I might need to make a move soon."

"Please stay a little longer."

Looking at me, she laughed. "You keep negotiating with me, Mike."

It was true, I kept negotiating with her and wanted her to stay longer. Maybe I was falling in love slowly and did not know how to express my feelings, and for sure could not stop them from invading my heart.

"Yes, I am and I do not want you to leave yet. I want to know you better."

She looked into my eyes and challenged me. "What do you want to know about me?"

"Everything!" I gave a charming smile, exaggerating, and making funny faces.

"That's a lot, Mike!" she laughed.

"OK, OK, let's start slowly. What is your favourite sport?"

"Well, believe it or not, basketball, but I am no good at it. I mostly walk. Not much with sport, in a way. What about you?"

"Swimming, and I am trying to go once or twice a week for a swim."

As I asked more and more I found out we both liked the same worship songs and we had fun playing the question game of knowing each other.

"What do you think about our Tuesday group?"

Looking at her, I felt pretty confident. "It is something new to me, but all the Bible studies and prayers work for me and I feel I am growing closer to the Lord and closer in adoration to Him, and it is good. I am actually developing a relationship with the Lord; learning how to ask in prayer, surrender, listen and follow the Lord, even when I don't understand."

"I love the prayers. Emma is very good at guiding prayer time."

Looking down, I was not sure how to start. "Do you think you could back me up in a special prayer?" Looking at me, Bella waited for me to continue. I went into the lounge and brought a notebook and opened it. "This is my sorry list; is a list the Lord put on my heart to make, and to pray about certain people." Hesitating, she was not sure about looking, but I sat next to her and showed her. "I did speak with John and my mum, but only with you I am sharing this notebook page now. I want to share it with you." She was quiet so I continued. "I moved ahead with so many things through prayer and following how the Lord guided me. However, I did not move forward with my father and Scott."

"So, this is something you did and asked the Lord to help you reconnect with some people from your past, like your father and brother?"

I acknowledged to her that in a way it is important to say I am sorry and ask for forgiveness and yes, reconnect!

"But you said you are meeting with them?"

Then I started to explain to her my family situation dynamics on my father's side, but this time there was not much pain–it was just the way it was–and I wanted to be different, better.

"Bella, you know what is hi and goodbye, and how are you? Simple conversations or deep conversations. My father was never fond of me and I was never much considered his son. I did manage to have a chat with him and he did say would like to get closer as a family. However, my mum warned me, and she was right. It is a process and I am just responsible for myself. I did my part and he is still on the same road. Not sure if we will really connect. Is up to the Lord." Looking down, I put my hand at my chest. "It was so painful in the past and I wish I could do something about it, but I really cannot do anything at all. And with Scott it is even worse. He did not even want to hear from my apologising, and I could not approach him at all for maybe a deeper connection."

"Mike, you mum is right, you did your best. It is also their choice if they do want to be friends with you and, you know, be a family. You cannot force someone to like you or love you. You can love them and stand next to them—it is your choice—if they let you. But you always can pray for them."

Mike put his head down, and was sad and was quiet. He was not speaking at all and Bella felt helpless. She was not sure if she wanted to be there. She did not expect a deep conversation at this level, and Mike opened all his heart to her.

"And I really wanted my dad to be proud of me, too. I never heard one word from him. It was always Scott, and Scott did not want to have anything to do with me and treated me like I was nobody. And I just wanted to be part of the family, and never was or will be. I tried to be the best brother and son I could ever be."

Bella put her hand over his shoulder. "It is good to give it all to God as your loving Father. You need to heal, Mike, a lot of healing, and you need to keep forgiving them and take one day at a time. And it will be fine. The Lord will carry you through everything."

He put his head on his knees and his arms, and he was crying quietly, and Bella touched his hair and was trying to calm him down and put her arms around his shoulders and her head on his back, and could feel his heart beating and his deep pain.
After a few minutes, he was calm and stood up and walked into the dining room without saying anything and returned with fresh drinks.

"I am sorry, I don't think I cried. You must think…" he said, smiling this time.

She stopped him and spoke kindly. "I do not think anything. I am a friend and your sister in Christ. It is OK to cry, Mike. I believe what you shared is very much deep into your heart."

"Yes, I did. Thank you, Bella!" and took her hand into mine and thanked her.

It was quiet for a moment and Bella spoke up. " I would like to pray for you, Mike. Is that all right?"

"That would be very good, Bella, thank you. I would love that."

She started praying a very beautiful prayer, and it was not so much the words for me – it was the peace and the joy I was receiving from the Father. It was something I did not do much before with someone alone, except with my mum when she asked me to. Before she left, she came near me and gave me a hug, and for a moment I held her tight. I wished she would not go.

"I will keep you in my prayers, Mike. I believe you need to take it a step at a time, and the Lord will guide you, and help you, and heal you."

"Thank you, Bella, for today. I really enjoyed it. Maybe we can meet another time."

"Yes, Mike, will see how the Lord leads," and she left, smiling.

Chapter 8
A season of rest

Since I met Bella it has been a couple of weeks and you would not believe that it was October, and yes, the smell of Christmas was near.

I was not sure how this Christmas would be for me. Past years I spent it with my mum and she was very kind to me, and then I would also visit John and Emma. And yes, Holly. How did I forget about Holly? Well, she was out of my life. And at this point in time I was not sure if I really wanted a girlfriend or not. But probably I was thinking more of Bella than before and had a more open mind for dating. And prayers do work, as I started to pray for the Lord to guide me.

These past weeks things started slowly to change, and my father made a bit of an effort and invited me for dinner and Molly, his wife, was nice and we had a lovely evening together. So I felt in a way I was in a good direction with my father – slowly. And all because of the mercy and grace of the Lord, which was working and making a way. The best I could do was resting at his feet and praying. But developing patience was slow, and waiting upon the Lord when you don't understand is not easy.

With Scott things were the same. No sign of him wanting to meet me or interact with me at all, so I just left it like this and I would occasionally send him a text message; kind of letting him know that I was alive and still here. And yes, pray and pray. Scott, as all of us, was in God's hands.

My heart slowly started to move forward and I was not in pain so much anymore. I was moving forward by letting the Lord work in my heart. I was moving further by surrendering the Lord and trusting him and leaning on him. I started getting involved at church with helping more, and I started to team with John by helping families that needed repairs or help over the weekend.

I did not forget about my other side of the family but started to "chill", as John said, and trust more and more that the Lord was working into the hearts of the loved ones.

Bella, yes, I did not forget Bella. I was actually praying for her daily. And even if I did not see her (only Sunday and Tuesday) to me was getting closer to my heart, in my heart, falling in love with her.

No, I was not sure about dating her. Maybe I admired her too much from a distance and did not know what to do. Maybe I felt it was too much for me. Anyway, I was not moving regarding Bella. I did not invite her over anymore, but being part of the Tuesday group I still met her as she was part of the same group, and that was good to see her. That was enough for me now. (Or I was in a cosy situation and did not want to move.)

It was a Tuesday evening and John asked me if I wanted to stay over for a cup of tea. Actually I said yes for some reason, even if I felt tired.

"So, what is going on with you, John?"

"Well, good news, good news!" he smiled, and as Emma walked into the dining room he said, "Shall we tell him?"

Emma looked at him as she took some books and said goodnight. "I am going upstairs, see you later, if I am not asleep." Then, looking at me, said to her husband, "Of course, John. He is a very close dear friend."

Looking shocked, I tried to figure out what is going on. "Please tell me you are not moving?" I got a bit scared as I did not want that to happen.

"No, guess again! We are going to have a baby!"

I looked a bit puzzled and took me some time to get the news. "A baby! That is great news!"

"Well, it was like a miracle as we almost lost hope! But God is good and faithful and blesses us when least expected."

"Yes, I know you mentioned that the doctors did not give a positive feedback for you two to have a baby. But that is great. Someone else on my list to pray about."

John smiled and nodded. "She is nine weeks, and yes, it is great. We are so overwhelmed by God's goodness. Now, what about you, Mike?"

"Me? Just me and my work and church. You know I love pairing with you, and keep helping you on

Saturdays sometimes when we help some family with DIY and repairs."

John brought more coffee and insisted on an area where I did not want to go: Bella.

"I can see the way you connect with Bella and I was wondering if you will make the move and ask her out for a date?"

Looking tired, as I heard those words before, and not wanting to dig deep down in my heart, I still answered my friend. "That is a very good question, John. But I am sure she is busy. And I do pray for her. I do not know what to do, honestly. I did not think of it."

"Well, I do know she likes you and she is praying for you too. What stops you?"

I insisted, a bit disarmed, "I do not know. I have no clue even how to ask her out."

John laughed. "You had few girlfriends, and you tell me you lost your touch. The last one, Holly, she ran after you a few times. Well?"

"Do you think I should ask her out?"

John added, "If *you* do not ask her, probably Mark or some other guy will ask her. She did meet other young people from church. If I were you, I would pray and try. What can you lose? At least you will know if it is an open door from the Lord or not. I don't want to see you end up alone!"

As I left, I was thinking of what John said and did not really know how to process it. Maybe tomorrow I will have a fresh thought about it.

Next day I started my morning with prayers and then was busy at my work, and the day was flying.

As I was ready to leave home I got a message from Bella:

Hi, Mike, how are you? I was wondering if I can ask you a favour? It is my mum's birthday coming up and I was wondering if you can make something for her out of wood. If I am asking too much, it is OK. Don't worry. God Bless. Bella.

That was a pleasant surprise and replied to her:

Hi, Bella, so lovely to hear from you. Yes, it would be my pleasure to make something for her. Do you want to come around this week? Could show you some of my little carvings. God bless. Mike.

Yes, I can be at your house at 11.30am Saturday and have some lunch together. Is it on me, I think.

I agreed and felt quite good about meeting her as I had not really met her in quite some time—just me and her—and wanted to know how she was doing.

She came on Saturday and I was so happy to see her. As she came in she was very nice and brought me a little cactus plant. I looked a bit surprised and she explained to me that it does not need a lot of water and hopes I will keep it as she noticed I did not have any plants. True, I was not very much with plants and did not know what to do with them, but was very grateful for her thoughtful gift. I was thinking about naming the little cactus plant Bella and it made me smile. I asked her what did she had in mind for lunch.

"What do you say if we actually go out for late lunch or early dinner? I know a very good Chinese restaurant near me, and like this I can go straight home.

"That will be fine with me!"

I looked at her and she looked tired. "How are you, Bella?" I sat on the opposite couch in the conservatory looking at her, a bit concerned!

She looked down for a moment and took a big deep breath. "My mum had been in hospital with a hip replacement and I had to look after her a lot over the past few weeks and feel really tired lately. Actually, I could do with a good sleep. But coming to her birthday I thought that you could make something nice for her. I really love the nice lotus flower you gave me."

I looked at her and sat next to her with a big book that I took from one of the little shelves. "This is a book with a lot of designs and images from nature. Do you want to choose one? There are some ideas and sometimes they help me to create, or I try to work on some piece I never thought of."

Bella looked at the pages and admired them. "They are very beautiful. However, I thought maybe something like a Bible, open, very small, you know, and written a scripture on it. She loves the verses:

The joy of the Lord is my strength! Actually, they are one of my favourites too."

"That would be fine, no problem. I can finish them in a few days for next week maybe. Usually I work in the evenings, or when I can, depending on how I feel and how tired I am." I smiled.

"No rush, her birthday is a few weeks from now!"

I looked at her and she dropped the book on the floor and we both wanted to pick it up and we bumped heads.

"I am so sorry!" I laughed, and then as I touched her hand I dropped the book and took her hand into mine. "You know, Bella, you have been in my heart for some time. I had been praying and thinking of you."

She looked at me with big eyes, petrified in a way, not sure what she was thinking, then she got shy and spoke, whispering, "I had been praying for you, too."

"Look, Bella, I was thinking—" and before I could even start, her phone rang and it made me feel so bad as I was really ready to ask her for a date, believe it or not. It was quite unexpected, even for me. But somehow I got my courage and then got interrupted.

"I am sorry, Mike. I expect a phone call from my mother."

I stood up and felt a bit frustrated that the moment was gone, but managed to be polite. "It is OK, no problem. We can talk later," and I just walked into the kitchen and did a few things there.

She had a little chat on the phone and after a few minutes she approached me afterwards. "I am so sorry, you were going to say something?"

I got busy in the kitchen, mostly moving things around. "Yes, I was, but it does not matter." I was discouraged and tried to avoid her eyes.

"Oh but, Mike, it does matter." She seemed determined, and I turned around as I was in the kitchen and looked at her.

"Bella!"

She seemed a bit lost in thoughts and did not look at me.

"Bella!" I called her again and walked slowly toward her. She looked at me and was waiting for me to say something.

"I know I am not quite a perfect guy and not on the faith road for long. However, I want to go out with you. I would like you to be my girlfriend!"

For a moment she did not say anything and I wanted to say something else. She looked at me.

"Well, that is if you do not date anyone else. I would—"

Bella interrupted me. "I would love to go out with you, Mike. However, I want to take things slowly as I had my heart broken before and I am sure you went through a lot of things, and you shared some."

"Yes, Bella, will take a day at a time. Trust me, I do not want my heart broken again. And it would be good to start getting to know each other better." Deep down in my heart I did agree with her–step by step approach–especially after my dating experiences.

I turned around and spoke out of the blue, more for myself then for her. "That was easier than I thought!" and I heard her laughing.

"Did you think I would say no?"

The atmosphere started to chill a bit, and felt relaxed.

"Well, you know John and Emma were on our case for some time. And they are right, we need to try, however, I had to be ready and it took me some time."

"Yes, I know, it took me some time, too."

As we went out the door I gently took her by the hand and looked at her to see her reaction and she just smiled.

"I am not eating you, am I?"

"No, you are just beautiful, and I have no clue what I am doing."

"You are doing very well, Mike!" she encouraged me.

I looked at her and a thought crossed to my mind. "Am I? So can I kiss you today?" I laughed.

"There will be boundaries, you know! But yes, a kiss might be all right. Let's not rush!"

I stopped for a moment and changed the subject. "I am sorry, maybe rushing!"

We enjoyed the walk and then I asked her, "Tell me how your mother is?"

"She is home – resting. She is doing her little walking exercises. She has a very nice group of ladies, friends, who help her, visit her. But I also tried to help as much as I can."

We had a lovely evening out and it was great, I felt so good.

My phone rang later on and it was my mum.

"Hey, Mum, how are you?

"Hello, Mike, I am fine. I was thinking if you are still OK to meet me tomorrow at 4pm or you have other plans?"

I told her to wait a minute and then asked Bella, "Would you like to meet my mother tomorrow? I spend, usually, Sundays at 4pm onwards with her for a few hours – dinner and chatting. She is a lovely, kind lady."

"I would love to meet your mother. But I am checking on Mum after church tomorrow and hope to rest a bit. Sundays seem quite busy for me!"

I nodded yes and spoke with my mum. "Yes, it's fine, no problem. See you at 4pm. I will make a reservation at your favourite restaurant. "

"Thank you, Mike. See you tomorrow."

On the way back I noticed that Bella was looking very tired. "You look tired, Bella. Do you want me to drive you home?"

"Yes, please, would you mind?"

On the way back we listened to a lovely Christian song by Unspoken and soon enough I found myself speaking alone as she fell asleep in the car. It was quiet, and I loved driving with worship in the background and next to a lovely lady. In front of her house I asked her more, whispering, "Shall I take you inside?"

And she nodded, asleep.

"Where are your front door keys?"

"In my bag."

I opened the front door and took her gently in my arms and carried her upstairs. I had the cat with me showing me the way. She was still asleep, curling in my arms. She must have been so tired. I put her on top of the bed and covered her with a blanket. She was still holding, in a way, to me and I spoke gently. "You need to let me go. And you still owe me a kiss."

"Yes, no, all right." She was talking in her sleep.

"I wish I could stay, but maybe one day when we are married." I smiled, but I knew she would not hear, and then I turned off the light and kissed her on her cheek and before I left I wrote a note: *I will pick you up tomorrow morning for church, 9.45am. Mike*. I left the hall light on and turned on the lock of the door as I left, and drove off.

It would be great to see what my mum would say tomorrow, and all the church. Makes me smile just thinking of it. That evening I spent it just thanking God for all the blessings; thanking the Lord that even if I did not know how and what to do, He made a way for me to date Bella.

Chapter 9
Mothers

As I woke up in the morning I went into the past. My mind raced for some reason, thinking of my life. My life, from being a mess, started to make, slowly, sense and the Lord was guiding me in the right direction. It felt a slow process to me but also painful sometimes, but rewarding, and walking on a new path of grace and finding who I was. Also, I felt so blessed to have Bella in my life and not walk alone on this journey of life – to find true love. I was head over heels in love with her.

I picked up Bella from home and she smiled as she opened the front door. She was dressed in a very nice blue dress and had a cardigan, and her hair was on the shoulders.

"I can see you took care of me last night, you brought me home. That was sweet of you. I must have been so tired."

"Come on, Bella, you were so sweet as you fell asleep in the car."

As we drove toward church I started a deeper conversation which Bella was very surprised about. "I was wondering about you and your life, Bella."

"Yes, we have plenty of time to start knowing each other, no?"

I backed up a bit but still, curious continued. "Yes, however, it will be good to start with the basics. I believe you know more about me than I know about you."

"Fare point, Mike. All right, you can ask two questions for now, otherwise we will miss church."

"I was wondering about your job. Why did you become a teacher? And also why did you divorce?"

Bella looked at me and said, "Touché! You know what to ask. The shorter version is that I love working with children and teaching. I have always had that passion since I was a child, and my mum encouraged me in this path."

It was quiet and I looked at her as I was driving. She looked sad and then after a few minutes she said, with a lower voice, "Now, I told you a few things before about my past relationship. I married the wrong guy and had been in a very coercive relationship, and then two years later we divorced as he had somebody else. Through those times I drew near to the Lord and experienced forgiveness, healing and grace and an intimacy with the Lord."

"Oh. I am so sorry!"

She looked at me, and with her big green eyes she said, "Now, my turn! I know your family situation. What about your love life, Mike?"

"Touché!" I laughed. "Payback time, hey?"

"No, I just wanted to know a few things about you – on a deeper level."

I nodded with my head, and not quite proud of myself and making faces, spoke. "You want to go deeper about me, hey? I was a curious, cheeky boy. However, I managed to get a good job, good position as manager, but had two girlfriends when I was young and then got stuck up with Holly for a year. You would call it a relationship for convenience, and to live a life like the world does – like everyone. Felt so lost and had quite a sad love life – nonexistent. In a way I started to lose my identity and lost even touch with my hobbies. Till I had a dream with an angel some time ago that took me to church. Then I told John I want to go to church, and you know the rest. We met the same day, I think."

"Yes, I remember. And can I ask one more question?" and she looked very curious. "What made you decide to date me?"

From how anxious I was in the past months and where I was today, I came far away, but probably was not realising how much the Lord worked at my heart. Things that hurt me were memories and scars, and new ideas, new paths in the wilderness made by the Lord. I felt more secure in who I was and what I was seeking. "First time we spoke I felt peace, and each time when I was around you I felt joy and peace. I knew from the first time that I wanted to be with you, even if I did not know how to talk to you or behave near you. Then we met a few times and you were always kind to me. I really admire you and you are so wise, beautiful and patient. Which I am quite the opposite. I guess John kind of spotted that I like you and gently asked me a couple of times if I would make the move."

Bella smiled and continued my ideas. "Emma asked me if I liked you and enjoyed your company, too."

"We are almost at church. Now, why did you say yes to date me?" I wanted one more turn.

"I believe it is because I saw a very caring, gentle soul and very kind man. And you have been so helpful. Pretty handsome too."

"Still got the looks, baby!" We both laughed.

We were at church and I opened the car door for her and she came out. I took her by the hand and both walked toward the church.

"Are you ready?" I looked at her and was not sure what she was about to say, and before she could answer a few ladies walked toward us.

"Oh, how nice to see you Mike, Bella. Do you mind me asking, but are you dating?"

I looked at Bella and got the idea. Everyone that knew us would ask us if we are dating. At least we will have to get it through even if I found it a bit overwhelming, and Bella smiled shyly.

"Yes, we are." I smiled.

"That's so great, you look like such a lovely couple."

Once they left they told a few others and we both looked at each other and smiled. The chain of news was open and by the time we would be in the church everyone would know.

"Bella, Mike, lovely to see you." John patted me by my back.

I shook hands with him and he looked at us and, knowing John, he said, "I can see you got brave enough to ask her out!"

"Yes I did, finally, John! And she said yes."

"Very happy for you both!"

"Where is Emma?" asked Bella.

"Emma is in the church. Actually, you might find a chair or two next to her if you hurry. She would be so glad to see you two together. I believe you are a lovely couple and the Lord brought you together."

Walking toward Emma we knew what she would say and Bella whispered to me, "I think it is getting a bit embarrassing to me and too much."

"I know how you feel. Don't worry, it will be over soon."

After the service, we kind of left pretty early as we had enough of everyone smiling at us and asking us about dating. I drove her home and told her I will pick her up later.

"Mike, do you mind if you drive me to my mum's house? I promised to visit her today. I am sorry, I just remembered."

On the way there I saw a little Tesco Express and stopped and told her, "Wait, I will be back." As I walked in I bought three bouquets of flowers.

"Wow, that is amazing!" she said, as I entered the car a few minutes later.

I handed her a beautiful bouquet of roses that were red.

"Red – love! Aww! She looked at me, getting shy.

I came near her and looked into her eyes. "Well, do I get a kiss?"

"What for?" She looked at me, playing a game.

"I am crazy in love with you, come on."

She came near me and gave me a little kiss on the lips and then I took her gently by the waist and pulled her near me. It was a bit funny as we were both sitting in the car and I was ready to drive off. As she was so near me I kissed her gently and touched her face with my hand. She smelled like flowers and she was adorable.

"Cheeky. You are stealing kisses."

As we stopped in front of her mum's house, I said to Bella, "I have a bouquet of flowers for your mum and one for my mum. So all the ladies will be happy."

"Good. Would you mind meeting my mum? Her name is Grace Wilson."

As I entered the house following Bella, in a chair watching TV, very loud, was her mum. She looked a bit older than my mum. A very nice lady, and she smiled.

"Mum, this is Mike. I told you about him."

She looked at me a bit seriously and I was not sure how to make it out. Then she handed her hand and was polite.

"Nice to meet you, Mike. You are the one that stole my Bella."

"Yes, Mrs Wilson." And I gave her a bouquet of flowers, wishing her the best.

She stood up, walking with a stick slowly, and I offered my arm to help her walk. Bella smiled as she went into the kitchen to prepare some drinks.

"You are staying for a little lunch, are you?"

I looked at Bella and I nodded, not knowing what to do.

"Don't look at Bella. You are staying, Mike. Me and you need to know a bit about each other!"

She was so opposite from my mum–very chatty– and she told me all kinds of stories about how God did a lot of healing, and miracles in the church. After an hour or so she said, "Now, kids, I am tired. I have a friend coming over soon and I need to rest. Bella, I am quite happy that you have such a handsome, kind young man. And that he loves the Lord. Will talk on the phone."

I looked at Bella as she stood up and kissed her mum and gave her a hug. Grace looked at me and said, "Come, son, you can give me a hug too. And you can call me Grace!" and she gave me a tight hug and squeezed me.

We left and Bella said, "It is almost 2.30pm in the afternoon. What shall I do now?"

"Come at my house, since I was kind of set up with a visit for your mum. She is so different from my mum. Total opposite personality."

Bella made a face. "She is adorable, but does talk too much sometimes, and loves her stories of prayers and healing and church. I heard them so many times."

"She is lovely; is good to know your small family. And you are very patient listening to your mum."

She agreed to come to my house, and we snuggled on the couch and I turned on Netflix. We found a comedy and we watched for a while, and it was so quiet that you could hardly hear the movie, and I literally fell asleep, and she put her head on my chest and fell asleep as well. And the movie was still going on.

After some time, I heard a noise and moved, and heard my mum speaking to me. At the beginning I thought I was dreaming, but actually she was in my house.

"Hello, Mike. I knocked at the door, but no one opened and I knew you were home and saw your car, so I came in." She smiled and looked at me as I just woke up and realised Bella was asleep in my arms. I felt a bit embarrassed and my mum just smiled and made me embarrassed. Bella moved and opened her eyes, and looked a bit scared.

"I fell asleep, did I?"

"Me too!" I laughed, a bit of a funny way to introduced her to my mum. "This is Helena Davis, my mum. I carry her family name, which I chose, and actually and I am proud of it."

"Nice to meet you, Bella. I heard so many things about you."

"She is my lovely girlfriend, which is a blessing to me. I wanted to surprise you, and invited her to join us for dinner."

My mum really liked Bella. And who would not really like her as she was adorable. Probably they both had some similar personality; more quiet.

The afternoon passed quickly, and it was evening and I took Bella home.

It was such a blessed day for me and felt like a new beginning and that the Lord was so good to me. I felt that the Lord was opening doors of favour and things were slowly falling into place.

Now, Monday was a busy day, and Tuesday too, and me and Bella – we managed to meet and also talk on the phone each day, which was pretty good. The week passed very quickly and I was looking forward to spending my Saturday afternoon with Bella and to go somewhere. She came around lunchtime and I was so happy to see her, as during the week I did not have much time – just for a dinner meeting.

"Hey, Bella! I am so glad you are here!"

She was so patient with me as I started sharing about my busy week. I was trying to convince her again to get her a new car and she was not quite decided.

"Mike, that is sweet of you but I cannot really afford it, and I am kind of fond of my little car."

"Come on, Bella, let me take care of you!"

"Maybe. We will see. Give me some time. You go at a very quick speed sometimes."

"All right, all right. I do move very quickly, I am told all the time that at work." I backed off.

We went for a walk in the park and then we returned home as I wanted to drive Bella for dinner to a special place which I chose. We had a lovely time together and I felt like time was flying and

I really did not want to go home. I drove her home and it was very quiet in the car and she looked at me a few times. I finally dared to say few words. "You keep looking at me. Am I doing something wrong?"

"No, there is nothing wrong, Mike."

I looked at her and did not give up. "Well, are you going to tell me, or is it a secret?" I just parked the car and I stopped and turned toward her.

"I had a lovely evening and I did not feel so good in such a long time." She had a few tears coming down on the cheek and hid her face in her hands. "I am sorry, I am a bit emotional," she whispered.

I put my arms around her and held her tight. "Bella, you are really adorable, even when you cry. You cannot imagine how much my life has changed since I met you. You bring the best out of me."

She got out of the car quickly and I jumped after her and followed her till the door. She turned around and I was so close to her. She curled into my arms and said nothing. I could feel her heart's bits and feel her breath, and she smelled like roses. "Bella, I had an amazing evening, thank you."

She was ready to go inside and she smiled. "I never believed I would meet someone as kind as you."

Drawing near her, I looked at her and touched her face gently and kissed her. But this time she was not any kind of woman, but a woman that I fell in love with, and so sweet and gentle soul. I found my soulmate when I did not expect or plan, and the Lord had been so good to me. She was my princess and I was head over heels in love with her.

Chapter 10
The test of Love

Sunday passed pretty quickly in a way and church was uplifting as usual. However, when I came home things turned around so quickly and I could not really believe it. I was not prepared for it and it was so unexpected. But life would be boring if we would not be challenged and if we would have a perfectly planned life. We learn when we are challenged, we grow when we move further and find ourselves in situations that make us move forward and stretch us, and we are doing things we never believed we were capable of doing.

Bella was supposed to come around 2pm as we talked about spending the afternoon together. I left late (church) and as I got home my phone rang and it was unexpectedly my father.

"Hey, Mike. How are you?"

"I am fine, Dad, fine. How are you?"

"Look, I know we are supposed to meet but I am a bit slow–you know me–but do not forget about you."

"It is OK, Dad," and looking at the clock, any time Bella would be here, and if my father was in the mood for a long conversation that was not the best timing, but did not want to cut him short as it was so hard to catch him and have a chat with him.

"Maybe you can come around next week with your girl, as I've heard you found yourself a nice lady."

"Yes, her name is Bella, as I told you, Dad. And thank you for the invite, we would love to come."

It was quiet for a moment and my dad and I thought he would finish the conversation, but he said with a slow voice, "Look, son, I called you also to… tell you, that Scott was involved in a car crash and he is in, well, at the hospital. They just called me and I do not know what to do."

For a moment everything stopped and felt the time and space and the world froze and my heart felt like it was going to explode. "When did it happen?" I've asked my father.

"They called me an hour ago. He is not in a coma, but he was injured, they told me. I do not know what to do, Mike!" He started to melt.

I could hear in my father's voice that he was emotional and he was probably shaking. Molly was heard in the background talking and encouraging him.

"Dad, let me call the hospital and see what's going on. And maybe we can go for a visit. All right, Dad? Then will call you back. Dad, do not worry, will be fine; will pray for him."

"Thanks, son. Call me if you know anything, all right? I will wait for your call."

As I hung up the phone I felt I was crashing down and literally fell on the couch, not being able to process it. I was not sure if I was in shock and panic, but was not able to move for a while – more like petrified. I felt a really deep pain in my heart and did not understand it; could not pray and could not move, was in total shock, could not even think.

I heard a noise, the main door opening, and I saw Bella walking in and then looking at me. She worried, and she rushed and came near me.

"Are you all right, Mike? What is wrong?"

After few minutes when I was back to normal I added, "My brother is in the hospital. Scott was taken to the hospital after a car crash."

She put her arms around me but I could not move. She was praying over me and felt peace covering me and stayed quiet at Jesus's feet. It was a precious moment then, like getting strength, I stood up and said, "I will need to call the hospital. I spoke with my father and said that I will try to find out what is going on."

"All right, Mike. If you want, we can order a takeaway."

I picked up the phone and dialled the hospital and a few minutes later I knew more than before and looked at Bella. "I am so sorry, Bella. This is quite a shock for me and not easy to handle."

"It is all right, Mike. We are here for each other. What did the hospital say?"

"Well, he has been injured and he is not in a coma, but sleeping a lot, which is good. However, his legs have been injured and will have to do some tests tomorrow. Once I call my father–hopefully he will not keep me for a long time–we will get out of the house. It would be good to take a lovely walk, don't you agree? I think fresh air would do good to me."

"All right, I just don't want you not to worry."

I was not worrying anymore and really enjoyed a lovely time with my Bella, and then home again.

As I promised my father, I tried to organise a visit at the hospital and actually I kept my promise. From then on, I visited Scott regularly. I would sit on the chair and look at him and it would feel like nothing changed; not so much his condition, but between us – me and him. I would feel sad sometimes, but hopeful. I brought a book which I started to read to him. It was something like *Stories for Children* (he used to love them when we were kids). He was mostly asleep, and then occasionally would say just hello to me and go back to sleep. I would always try to have a positive attitude with him and visit him every other day. The doctors were encouraged to see Scott, each day, getting better.

It was a Saturday afternoon, almost two weeks since the terrible event and he felt so good. He would not talk to me when I visited and he would not engage with me (even if the nurses told me that they engaged with him and spoke, and even my dad said he spoke a few words with him.

Something was happening with Scott and I could not understand it or explain it. It was something that would later on have an impact on his life but at this point he would not know it or see it. And I did not realise it or see it coming, either.

In a way, he was behaving that he did not want me to be there, but I would faithfully go and visit with him each day. He kind of avoided me or ignored me–I was not sure–but the majority of times would not bother me. I was there! He was able to sit up in his bed but he was not able to walk. He was a doctor himself so he had a pretty good idea what was going on. I would always be polite and smile and tell him things.

"Hi, Scott, how was your day?" and not hearing an answer would continue after a pause with my kind voice (as Bella said). "My day was pretty busy and I was thinking about coming and seeing you. We had a few good cars today. I know you would like that black Mercedes, which we got in today."

Today I felt a bit sad and did not feel quite up for it. It started to get tiring for me to keep coming and talking to him and he would not engage with me. I just wanted him to know I was there for him and did not know how to express it. Sometimes words were hard for me.

Today I had to say it as best as I could. "Look, Scott, I am coming to see you because you are my brother and I wished we would have had a better relationship. So, if you do not want me to come, tell me. I just wanted you to know I am here for you." With my head down and being discouraged, I stood up and was walking toward the door, already giving up, when I heard Scott saying with a soft voice:

"Mike, please stay!" and he did not look at me or say anything else for the rest of the day.

That was unexpected for me as I felt like giving up and he would not say more than hello and goodbye. I turned around and did not say anything to him, and stayed. I carried on reading to him from a book and telling him a little news, and then I left. For the first time in such a long time I felt I made progress. Well, to me it seemed very slow, but the Lord was working his plans and he was guiding me step by step. The Lord has his plan and that did not include one person, but all of us. And His plan, even if we did not understand it all the time, was best.

Next day, Scott was actually in a chair when I went to visit him.

"Hi, Scott."

And for my surprise he answered back pretty quickly, "Hi, Mike!"

We seemed to move somewhere, and I did not want to sound like I was pushing him.

Bella told me that it might not be best to visit him so often and the same thing was said by my best friend John. Probably they were right as I desired from all my heart to try to fix the past and try to help him but I felt I was not. I guess they were right and Scott needed his own time for healing and himself, and my visiting all the time might have been overwhelming for him. So, for the next few days, I did not go to the hospital to visit my brother. It was a decision that I took based on the fact that I was learning to surrender it all to the Lord and also out of respect for my brother, as though he might want a break from me. I was still wrestling with the Lord as I would have liked to have a relationship with my brother, but leaving it at Jesus's feet was not easy sometimes.

That day, as I walked in, Scott looked at me. He was so much taller than me and with dark hair. Pretty handsome, my brother! His big brown eyes looked at me as soon as I came in and the first thing he said was, "Why are you late? I have been waiting for you for the past four days."

I did not know how to react and what to make of it and said, surprised, "I was busy. Well, I was thinking not to come so often and to give you a break from me!"

He pretended he did not hear that and tried to move in his chair and could not do much. "How was your day?" He tried to make conversation.

That was quite a lot for Scott to speak with his brother, but for some reason he was making an effort and Mike realised that. He did not speak much more but Mike did share about his day at work as usual.

Before leaving Scott said, "I am starting my therapy tomorrow." He looked straight at Mike.

It was quiet, and a small goodbye and a sadness felt into Mike's heart. He prayed on the way home, and as he entered his house he felt lonely and he went straight to the shower. Then he went straight to bed. He was not sure he really wanted to go again to visit his brother, and find it difficult to keep seeing his brother like that; was not sure if he liked him with his proud, stubborn attitude, but he did not like to see him really struggling and suffering. He managed to be there for him as a brother, and felt things were moving in the right direction but still did not see any change in Scott's behaviour. In his defence, he spoke more than hi, which was good, but maybe not enough for developing a deep relationship. Actually, it was more like the beginning of a simple friendship.

It was another day tomorrow and he was meeting Bella. The night passed pretty quick and, being sad and praying, he fell asleep and woke up rested. He still had a sadness in his heart but made a decision. He felt the Lord wanted to prompt him to slow down visiting Scott. Actually, the Lord already prompted him many times, but we all get stubborn in listening to the Lord, obeying or pretending that we did not hear and try a way to get out of it by doing it ourselves, our own way. And when that happens the Lord is the one that turns all our mistakes into something good and shows us over and over grace and love.

The day passed pretty quickly and he was looking forward to meeting Bella. He was so preoccupied so much with Scott that each time when he met her he spoke about his brother. First thing when he met her he apologised. "Hey, Bella, how are you?" He gave her a quick kiss (he was picking her up from her house). He was looking at her. "You are so beautiful and I forgot how lovely you are. I am sorry, Bella. The past couple of weeks I had been quite absorbed with my brother and maybe I did not give so much attention to our relationship."

Bella looked at him and, with slow movements, touched his face. "Is all right. I know it has been a difficult period and I am standing by you, Mike. Wounds are healing hard and I know you want to help your brother. However, you still managed to look after me!"

He had a few tears in his eyes and came near her and put his hands around her. "You're so lovely!" and he held her tight in his arms and did not let go of her.

She felt touched by his cuddle and they stayed like this, connected into one lovely heart, in love with each other and being there for each other. It was a beautiful evening and Mike was laughing and Bella too and their faces were shining with love and their eyes had sparkles. He was finally on the right track by moving on with his life and surrendering all and trusting in the Lord and his ways, and accepting wherever the Lord was about to bring with his brother.

On Friday Mike decided to visit Scott again as he was not there for a few days now. But in his heart he felt good as he took a break and felt refreshed and ready to see his brother again. The Lord was taking both brothers on their own journey.

As he was walking toward his hospital room a nurse told him he was in the therapy room. He was directed toward there, and as he walked there and approached the door, stopped in front of it. With the back toward him was Scott walking and he could see through the windows his brother struggling. He was between two bars on each side and he was trying to walk. He was moving slowly, one leg and then another, and he was in pain and he tried again. Over the past weeks Scott lost some weight and he looked a bit changed.

Mike opened the door and silently approached through the back when he saw his brother pushing so hard, and he let go of a scream as he was in pain and was falling down. That moment, Mike was there and caught him from the back before he fell. The nurse brought the wheelchair and both put Scott into it.

Scott looked at Mike and, with a very firm loud voice that sounded angry, he said, "Why did you do that? I don't need your help."

Mike could not look at him and for a moment was silent. Then he looked straight into his eyes and with a soft voice added, "Because you are my brother and we are family and we are here for each other. So, I was here for you." He had tears in his eyes, ready to fall, and then he turned around and before he left he said, "You are right, Scott! You did not need my help, or you didn't need or want me to be here." I could not stay longer there as I felt I did my part and should not be there. I finally surrendered all to the Lord, and was out of my hands and out of my reach – my brother. I tried so hard for the past months to show him that I was a good brother and there for him, but he did not want to be a brother to me or a friend. It was time for me to let go and fully trust the Lord. I felt peace in my heart that I did my best and did it out of desire to make things right and how the Lord put on my heart.

Maybe one day Scott will understand this, maybe not, but my heart is finally free and could move on from the so-called "I am sorry list!" I finally realised that it was about me and my heart; about forgive and let go. And it was up to the Lord if he would reconcile some relationships, like with my father's side of the family, or not. I understood that I could not change the past and live in sorrow, condemnation, and guilt. The Lord wanted me to have a better life in Christ, and could make a better future by moving on with the Lord and trusting in him and accepting his will when he closed and opened doors.

Chapter 11
Brothers for life!

It was midweek and the weekend passed, and Bella and I had been visiting with my father. That had been such an encouraging time and his relationship with the father seemed to be getting better. He was trying his best and was pretty good and consistent. Well, it takes time to change, and no matter how hard we try to change, it is like we fall down and get up and fall down and feel we are getting nowhere. And even if we are, it is hard work and struggle all our life. But with the Lord, the journey is different as it is a journey of patience, transformation. He is kind and gentle and works at our hearts and circumstances. That is not only us; including everything and everyone around us. Even if sometimes the circumstances do not change immediately we do, because the Lord does change us and transforms us. The Lord is patient with us and loves us and wants to work his righteousness in us, his best in us, his grace and love in us.

I knew that it would take time to wire again with my father and I had to develop patience, and I started on the right journey by asking in prayer, wisdom and patience for myself and also praying for my father. My life since I was walking with the Lord was different and slowly I was learning to walk on the new path. I was learning to pray and ask, and how to listen and follow the Lord. I was developing a relationship with my loving Father. A relationship of trust, and surrender it all and take a step at the time. This was a bit hard for me, listening, but I was doing a pretty good job. Listening and following the spirit, no matter what, was brilliant. It was good on one hand, but on the other hand I felt stretched in every area of my heart, mind and soul. I felt challenged, and I felt on an adventure and felt carried through things I never imagined I would be able to do.

Yes, today I was visiting my brother again. I had a few days off over the weekend. But this time I was not anxious about visiting or not. I had peace in my heart and did my best and just followed the Lord. I was a new Mike with a new attitude and renewed mind.

The interesting thing is that I did not plan actually visiting him anymore and had no set-up day when I would. But earlier in the week I received a phone call from the hospital that Scott showed an interest in seeing me and asked me to visit him. If it would have been a few weeks ago I would have been surprised, but now, I was just visiting him without expecting anything in return; just trying to show him kindness and visiting because he asked me too, not because I was planning to go.

As I entered his room, something was different. He was sitting in the chair and he seemed anxious.

You could see his hands being tensed and also his face looked worried. As soon as I walked through the door he looked straight at me and, with a very direct and firm voice, he said, "Where have you been?"

I looked puzzled at him and did not know how to react, and for a moment I was astonished and stood still.

"I had been waiting for you. You did not come on Saturday for so many days!" Scott carried on.

"No, I did not. Come on, Scott, I know when I am not wanted or needed." I spoke calmly.

Scott did not say anything for a moment, then he started shaking and shivering and, with tears ready to fall from his eyes, looking at me he continued. "Nobody ever cared much for me in my life. But you… *you*!" He pointed at me, and looking straight at me he continued. "You, Mike – I did not treat you nicely when I started my job at the hospital. Mike, kind and gentle, my little brother. You came every day and stood by me. You showed me kindness and that you care in a way nobody did. You just came and had been here for me and asked nothing much! You stood by me when I felt so lonely and broken, and you showed me you are a true brother and that is what I did not do. I didn't do it when I was a child and for sure not now. I am sorry, Mike. I am so sorry for the way I treated you." And he put his head on his hands and started to cry and cry.

That was not something I would have imagined or thought would happen. Scott did look broken and nothing of the man I knew he was. I stood next to him and put my hands around him and gave him a hug. As much as a man I was, I had tears in my eyes and cried too with him as I never saw my brother in my entire life crying.

"Is OK, Scott. We are brothers, after all. I am not upset with you. I forgive you. I just wanted to be here for you. If you let me, Scott. If not, I understand. You have your life! The only thing I wished for is to be your brother!"

Scott looked at me and tried to smile, and had a differed attitude. "I want to be a better brother for you and I want you to stay please, Mike."

That was something that maybe wished for so long that I forgot, in a way. We both looked at each other and smiled, and felt like a new beginning and bond was between us. Then, trying to up the atmosphere, I changed the subject:

"So, what are you up to, Scott?"

"Well, I have already done my little walk and I am better. Do you think you can come next time to see how I am doing? Hope to go home next week."

"Will try my best, if you tell me what time it is. I might be able to squeeze a little break."

A nurse came with dinner and I brought the little table in front of him and Scott started to enjoy the meal, and suddenly he looked at me and gave me a slice of bread.

"Take some, Mike, you must be hungry."

"No, it's OK, it's fine."

"Please, Mike, I would like to share my dinner with you; would be an honour, my brother." He accentuated the word "my brother".

I took the bread, and in my heart I felt so touched by this new brother I had and it was something that I could not explain and was something new between us. "Oh, let me tell you: Bella and I went to see Dad last weekend."

"Did you? And how is our dad doing? And lovely Molly?" He smiled and we talked like two best friends.

"Well, he is trying harder, and they both love Bella. She has a patience and a touch for working with children and people. I am better with cars." I laughed.

"Yes, I am really happy for you, Mike. You finally seem to find yourself a nice girl, and you go to church as well. You seem to be on the right track."

Noticing that Scott was getting cold as the window was open, I went and closed the window and then I put his bathrobe around his shoulders. He touched my hand and smiled, and our eyes met. "Brothers for life?"

I looked at him and agreed, and he shook my hand and we looked for each other for a moment. It was sealed. "Brothers for life!"

It was getting dark and outside there was fresh air, and cold rain was coming so abundant and felt like never stopping.

"Maybe you should go home, it is getting late."

"Yes, I am taking Bella out tonight and then home. Do you have any girlfriend around, Scott? I did not see any beautiful girl coming around to see you."

Scott looked at me, making a face. "Actually, not. I had been too busy with my job the past few years and could not keep a girl. Tried last year, and a few months managed to keep a girl next to me, then she flew. Well, I was always at work and honestly not sure I liked her and for sure not in love." Looking at me, he smiled. "You look so in love, Mike. I wish I could meet my true love, the woman of my dreams, one day."

"I will pray for you, Scott. And you will see, you will meet her, the woman of your dreams one day."

As I left that evening something was new, and my heart was filled with gratitude and grace. The Lord was amazing and I could not be more thankful for my brother. He really touched me, and everything that happened this evening between us, and he was my brother. He really was my brother. The lost brother was here, was back. He was really my brother. We were brothers for life. And what I tried to do, I could not do.

The Lord opened the doors and the Lord worked in his time, which I tried for years. All my pain was gone. Jesus died for me on the cross and took all my pain away and healed me. And all my past was in a different light. God's grace and love covered all and was working his will, not only in me, but in all the people around me. The Lord did the impossible and made a way to my brother's heart. The Lord was good, God, a loving Father, and we were on a new road and on a new friendship and bounded by a new connection, bounded by the Lord. Brothers for life!

Bible References
English Standard Version

Chapter 1

Romans 12:12
Rejoice in hope, be patient in tribulation, be constant in prayer.

Psalm 16:11
You make known to me the path of life; in your presence there is fullness of joy; at your right hand are pleasures forevermore.

Romans 14:17
For the kingdom of God is not a matter of eating and drinking but of righteousness and peace and joy in the Holy Spirit.

Romans 12:2
Do not be conformed to this world, but be transformed by the renewal of your mind, that by testing you may discern what is the will of God, what is good and acceptable and perfect.

Philippians 4:8
Finally, brothers, whatever is true, whatever is honourable, whatever is just, whatever is pure, whatever is lovely, whatever is commendable, if there is any excellence, if there is anything worthy of praise, think about these things.

Isaiah 40:31
But they who wait for the Lord shall renew their strength; they shall mount up with wings like eagles; they shall run and not be weary; they shall walk and not faint.

Philippians 4:6-7
Do not be anxious about anything, but in everything by prayer and supplication with thanksgiving let your requests be made known to God. And the peace of God, which surpasses all understanding, will guard your hearts and your minds in Christ Jesus.

Chapter 2

John 3:16
For God so loved the world, that he gave his only Son, that whoever believes in him should not perish but have eternal life.

Romans 10:9-10
Because, if you confess with your mouth that Jesus is Lord and believe in your heart that God raised him from the dead, you will be saved. For with the heart

one believes and is justified, and with the mouth one confesses and is saved.

Psalm 37:4-5
Delight yourself in the Lord, and he will give you the desires of your heart. Commit your way to the Lord; trust in him, and he will act.

2 Corinthians 5:17
Therefore, if anyone is in Christ, he is a new creation. The old has passed away; behold, the new has come.

Isaiah 43:19
Behold, I am doing a new thing; now it springs forth, do you not perceive it? I will make a way in the wilderness and rivers in the desert.

1 John 4:18
There is no fear in love, but perfect love casts out fear. For fear has to do with punishment, and whoever fears has not been perfected in love.

Lamentation 3:22-23
The steadfastness of the Lord never ceases; his mercies never come to an end; they are new every morning; great is your faithfulness.

Chapter 3

John 14:6
Jesus said to him, "I am the way, and the truth, and the life. No one comes to the Father except through me."

1 Peter 2:5
You yourselves like living stones are being built up as a spiritual house, to be a holy priesthood, to offer spiritual sacrifices acceptable to God through Jesus Christ.

Joshua 1:9
Have I not commanded you? Be strong and courageous. Do not be frightened, and do not be dismayed, for the Lord your God is with you wherever you go."

2 Timothy 1:7
For God gave us a spirit not of fear but of power and love and self-control.

Psalm 27:14
Wait for the Lord; be strong, and let your heart take courage; wait for the Lord!

Proverbs 3:5-6
Trust in the Lord with all your heart, and do not lean on your own understanding. In all your ways acknowledge him, and he will make straight your paths.

John 14:27
Peace I leave with you; my peace I give to you. Not as the world gives do I give to you. Let not your hearts be troubled, neither let them be afraid.

Chapter 4

John 12:24-25
Truly, truly, I say to you, unless a grain of wheat falls into the earth and dies, it remains alone; but if it dies, it bears much fruit. Whoever loves his life loses it, and whoever hates his life in this world will keep it for eternal life.

Matthew 11:28
Come to me, all who labour and are heavy laden, and I will give you rest.

Psalm 56:3-4
When I am afraid, I put my trust in you. In God, whose word I praise, in God I trust; I shall not be afraid. What can flesh do to me?

Acts 2:38
And Peter said to them, "Repent and be baptised everyone of you in the name of Jesus Christ for the forgiveness of your sins, and you will receive the gift of the Holy Spirit.

Galatians 3:26
For in Christ Jesus we are all sons of God, through faith.

John 3:5
Jesus answered, "Truly, truly, I say to you, unless one is born of water and the Spirit, he cannot enter the kingdom of God.

Matthew 18:20
For where two or three are gathered in my name, there am I among them.

Chapter 5

Colossians 3:13
Bearing with one another and, if one has a complaint against another, forgiving each other; as the Lord has forgiven you, so you also must forgive.

Ephesians 4:32
Be kind to one another, tenderhearted, forgiving one another, as God in Christ forgave you.

Philippians 4:13
I can do all things through him who strengthens me.

Jeremiah 17:14
Heal me, O Lord, and I shall be healed; save me, and I shall be saved, for you are my praise.

Isaiah 53:5
But he was pierced for our transgressions; he was crushed for our iniquities; upon him was the chastisement that brought us peace, and with his wounds we are healed.

Psalm 41:3
The Lord sustains him on his sickbed; in his illness you restore him to full health.

Ephesians 2:8
For by grace you have been saved through faith.
And this is not your own doing; it is the gift of God.

<u>Chapter 6</u>

Jeremiah 29:11
For I know the plans I have for you, declares the
Lord, plans for welfare and not for evil, to give you a
future and a hope.

1 Peter 5:10
After all you have suffered a little while, the God of
all grace, who has called you to his eternal glory in
Christ, will himself restore, confirm, strengthen, and
establish you.

Philippians 4:19
And my God will supply every need of yours
according to his riches in glory in Christ Jesus.

Ephesians 3:20-21
Now to him who is able to do far more abundantly
than all that we ask or think, according to the power
at work within us, to him be glory in the church and
in Christ Jesus throughout all generations, forever
and ever. Amen.

Proverbs 22:4
The reward for humility and fear of the Lord is riches
and honour and life.

Proverbs 15:22
Without counsel plans fail, but with many advisers they succeed.

John 8:32
And you will know the truth, and the truth will set you free.

Chapter 7

John 4:24
God is spirit, and those who worship him must worship him in spirit and truth.

John 16:13
When the Spirit of truth comes, he will guide you into all the truth, for he will not speak on his own authority, but whatever he hears he will speak, and he will declare to you the things that are to come.

Psalm 145:18
The Lord is near to all who call on him, to all who call on him in truth.

Psalm 50:15
And call upon me on the day of trouble; I will deliver you, and you shall glorify me.

John 15:13
Greater love has no one than this, that someone lays down his life for his friends.

Proverbs 27:17
Iron sharpens iron, and one man sharpens another.

Proverbs 18:24
A man of many companions may come to ruin, but there is a friend who sticks closer than a brother.

Chapter 8

1 Corinthians 13:4-8
Love is patient and kind; love does not envy or boast; it is not arrogant or rude. It does not insist in its own way; it is not irritable or resentful; it does not rejoice at wrongdoing, but rejoices with the truth. Love bears all things, believes all things, hopes all things, endures all things. Love never ends. As for prophecies, they will pass away; as for tongues, they will cease; as for knowledge, it will pass away.

1 John 4:8
Anyone who does not love does not know God, because God is love.

Colossians 3:14
And above all these put on love, which binds everything together in perfect harmony.

1 Peter 4:8
Above all, keep loving one another earnestly, since love covers a multitude of sins.

1 Corinthians 16:14
Let all that you do be done in love.

2 Corinthians 5:17
Therefore, if anyone is in Christ, he is a new creation. The old has passed away; behold, the new has come.

Isaiah 43:19
Behold, I am doing a new thing; now it springs forth, do you not perceive it? I will make a way in the wilderness and rivers in the desert.

Chapter 9

2 Thessalonians 3:16
Now may the Lord of peace himself give you peace at all times in every way. The Lord be with you all.

Matthew 5:9
Blessed are the peacemakers, for they shall be called sons of God.

Colossians 3:15
And the peace of Christ rules in your hearts, to which indeed you were called in one body. And be thankful.

Psalm 4:8
In peace, I will both lie down and sleep; for you alone, O Lord, make me dwell in safety.

1 Peter 5:7
Casting all your anxieties on him, because he cares for you.

Galatians 6:9
And let us not grow weary of doing good, for in due season we will reap, if we do not give up.

Hebrews 12:1
Therefore, since we are surrounded by so great a cloud of witnesses, let us also lay aside every weight, and sin which clings so closely, and let us run with endurance the race that is set before us.

Chapter 10

Proverbs 17:17
A friend loves at all times, and a brother is born for adversity.

Colossians 3:12-13
Put on then, as God's chosen ones, holy and beloved, compassionate hearts, kindness, humility, meekness, and patience, bearing with one another and, if one has a complaint against another, forgiving each other; as the Lord has forgiven you, so you also must forgive.

1 Peter 3:8
Finally, all of you, have unity of mind, sympathy, brotherly love, a tender heart and a humble mind.

James 1:19
Know this, my beloved brothers: let every person be quick to hear, slow to speak, slow to anger;

Romans 12:15
Rejoice with those who rejoice, weep with those who weep.

Psalm 103:13
As a father shows compassion to his children, so the Lord shows compassion to those who fear him.

Romans 12:10
Love one another with brotherly affection.
Outdo one another in showing honour.

Chapter 11

Exodus 20:12
Honour your father and mother, that your days may be long in the land that the Lord your God is giving you.

1 Thessalonians 5:16-18
Rejoice always, pray without ceasing, give thanks in all circumstances; for this is the will of God in Christ Jesus for you.

Ephesians 6:18
Praying at all times in the Spirit, with all prayer and supplication. To that end, keep alert with all perseverance, making supplication for all the saints,

Matthew 6:6
But when you pray, go into your room and shut the door and pray to your Father who is in secret. And your Father who sees in secret will reward you.

Romans 8:26
Likewise the Spirit helps us in our weaknesses. For we do not know what to pray for as we ought, but the Spirit himself intercedes for us with groanings too deep for words.

Matthew 7:7
Ask, and it will be given to you; seek, and you will find; knock and it will be opened to you.

John 15:7
If you abide in me, and my words abide in you, ask whatever you wish, and it will be done for you.